EMERALD
OF
WISDOM

Forbidden Conflicts
~~ Book Five ~~

ANN M PRATLEY

BY ANN M PRATLEY

Forbidden Conflicts Series
Amethyst of Youth
Ruby of Law
Diamond of War
Sapphire of Prejudice

Power Moore Investigation Tales
Hoonigan
Resolution of Happiness
Home by the Sea
Tiger in Our House

Freedom of Flight Series
Christian
Brandon
Trinity

Painful Deliverance Series
Painful Deliverance
Darkness of Heart
Friendship of Desire

Golden Desires Series
The Golden Desires
The Golden Supremacy
The Golden Unity

Chisholm Manor Series
Alessandra

CHAPTER 1

As Vic Stonewarden stood under the hot flow of water in his apartment's shower, his mind was active. In three hours, he would be doing yet another job for his family. Since he'd turned nineteen, he'd been well trained and had gained exceptional experience in high-caliber jewelry theft. That was his family legacy. Stonewarden ancestors had been trusted to be wardens of gems. Over time, the literal interpretation of that had changed. Nobody in his current family dynamic had ever guarded jewels. What they did instead was take them. Take them, process them to sell in different forms, and then use the money gained from the sale to help others in need. It sounded romantic and good, robbing from the rich and giving to the poor. He knew the law would never see it that way.

The job they were about to do wasn't anywhere near the caliber of many they'd done before. It was only a small jewelry shop, and the gems were less well known than some that the Stonewardens had gathered over the years. What set the job apart for Vic was that it would be the first time that he'd run a job. It was long overdue, and he was ready for it, but it seemed like a very long time since he'd expected his father, Mitchell, to hand over control of the family business. There was still a long way to go before that happened completely, but the process had begun. It was what Vic had wanted for years. Now that he was about to do the first job without his father right beside him and his brothers, he began to feel overwhelmed. Was he ready? Was he in the right place to make sure everything went as smoothly as it should? Was he confident enough to be able to ensure it could all go to plan?

Things not going to plan wasn't something that would be new if it happened. There had been plenty of jobs that Vic had worked on, when things had either been a little bit too close in them getting caught, or so wrong in how it felt that they'd canceled and walked away rather than risk something going wrong. He knew that those scenarios were perfectly acceptable. No gems were worth risking the lives of family members for, no matter what.

The lives of his family - that was what drove him on in his nervousness in the lead up to the current job. By taking the lead, he'd effectively be taking responsibility not only for his own life, but also those of his younger brothers - James, Regan, Max, and Fitz. The skills they all had in heists was something to be confident about. They'd all been trained well by their father, Mitchell, whose military background had provided him with the appreciation for precision and worst-case scenario planning that worked well on the jobs. The Stonewarden sons had learned from the best, but could they really pull off such a job without Mitchell being right there with them while it happened?

In a moment of uncertainty, Vic moaned out loud. Was he doing the right thing? Was he sure he was ready? He had to take time to concentrate and get his head in the right space. Not doing so could surely contribute to disaster.

When he'd turned off the shower and stepped out to towel off, he took some time to wipe the bathroom mirror and then stand still, looking at himself. What he was going to be responsible for was something that he'd desired for years. He knew he had the maturity to guide his brothers in each of their roles. He knew he had the patience and the intelligence to assess if something about their plan wasn't sound. He knew he had years of training from his father. The unknown that hadn't yet been tested was whether Vic truly *was* all of those things when under the added pressure of being in charge.

"Babe, are you okay? It's already six," he heard his long-time partner, Hayley, call out to him.

Hearing her voice, Vic was forced to consider that if anything went wrong on the job, he and his brothers weren't the only ones who'd be affected. Hayley had been in his life for a decade. Over that time, she'd accepted the initial randomness of when Vic had to disappear for nights at a time to prepare for a job that his father would have been running. Hayley had never asked where Vic went, or what he did. Vic knew he possibly could have gone on forever, not sharing any information about his family life with her. When they'd passed the five-year mark, he'd known it was only right to inform her about who he truly was. She'd had responsibilities herself. He'd expected and accepted that she might walk away upon hearing his news. To his relief, she hadn't.

"Thanks," he called back to her as he continued to look at the man in the mirror. He was having doubts, and he knew that had to stop. There was no room in what they did as a family, for nervousness or doubt. If the job didn't feel good, it was better to walk away. "You got this," he said quietly to his reflection. "You want it, and you got it."

After breathing in deeply to shift his mood and his thoughts, he opened the bathroom door.

"I was considering coming in to see if you were okay," Hayley said suggestively as she ran a finger down over his chest and belly.

Vic grinned at her before nudging her up against the hallway wall and kissing her passionately. When he was in his regular nine to five job, and when he was around his family, there was little that truly made him happy. When he was in the presence of the woman he loved, it was easy to smile.

"You can't be late," Hayley said as she felt him pull back. "But rest assured, lover - I'll be getting more of those kisses later!"

"Oh, yes you will," Vic said, continuing to smile as he made his way to the bedroom to dress.

He moved swiftly in putting on the clothing that wouldn't be too noticeable if he was seen around the area of the jewelry shop. Into a bag went other clothing for afterward. As a family, they had their routines and methods of getting in, getting what they wanted, and getting away. It wasn't always seamless, but he considered that they probably did incredibly well compared to most other criminals who chose theft as their form of income.

Criminals. He hated that word but knew it was accurate. At times, it didn't seem like a bad thing, what they did. Some people they'd robbed were so rich that the Stonewardens expected they might not even notice some of their jewels being missing. It probably wasn't a correct scenario, but thinking that helped to lessen the guilt after each job.

Walking out of the bedroom, he took time to locate Hayley and pull her into his arms.

"Be careful out there," Hayley said as she raised a hand and cupped the side of his face. "Come back in one piece, *please*."

Vic smiled and gently kissed her lips, taking a moment to center his thoughts again as he savored having such an incredible woman in his life.

"I will," he said as he pulled back slightly and

studied her face. "Tonight I'll be going with Dad to see what happens after a job, so I don't know how late I'll be…"

"No matter how late you are, please just take a few seconds at some point afterward to let me know that you're okay," Hayley said, her strength shining through the force of her words and tone.

"I will," Vic whispered before pulling her close one more time. "I'll see you later," he said as he turned and walked to the door of their apartment.

Hayley smiled and watched as the door opened and closed, leaving her alone. For a long while, she stood still, letting the same anxiety flow over her that she'd always felt since learning what Vic did out of family commitment and loyalty. The Stonewarden way of living wasn't something she'd seen before meeting him, but she knew he was a good man, even if he did break the law like he did. She knew it was part of being a Stonewarden. She also knew she had to accept it, because she certainly couldn't walk away from the man that she loved so deeply.

CHAPTER 2

Mitchell Stonewarden felt mixed emotions at what was to come that night. He'd been head of the Stonewarden business for so long, having taken it over not long before his father had died. That was how it usually worked - the leader decided when it was time to hand over control, and the next in line stood up. For hundreds of years, it hadn't been unlike the formation of a monarchy, except what the Stonewardens did wasn't anywhere near as glamorous or honorable.

As he waited for his final two sons to join the group in the living room of their large family home, he glanced around. Sitting on one of the big old armchairs was his second-oldest son, James. Not far away, sharing the three-seater sofa, were Max and Regan. They talked happily enough among themselves, but there was always something unnatural about their conversation with one another.

Since losing his wife, Caroline, a decade earlier, Mitchell had spent many hours watching and listening to his five sons, plus his daughter, Charlie. They were an interesting lot at times, but he was proud of each and every one of them. They were all a part of the Stonewarden family business in one way or another. They didn't all like it, but they all did it.

As his mind began to wander more into his memories of the long marriage he'd shared with Caroline, he heard the front door open. Into the lounge walked his oldest son, Vic, and his youngest son, Fitz. One looked as hyperactive as he always did when they did a job. There was no calming Fitz down on such nights. Mitchell could only appreciate that Fitz was also able to keep his eagerness in check when they worked.

"How are you feeling?" Mitchell asked Vic when everyone was seated.

"Yeah, I'm good," Vic replied. Inside, his heart was beating stronger and faster than usual, but he pushed it out of his thoughts. "Let's go over this one more time," he said as he turned and addressed his brothers.

As the five brothers moved closer around the coffee table where building structural plans were laid out, Mitchell relaxed back. He was there, and he was listening, but unless he heard something that could potentially result in disaster for the night, he wasn't going to say anything. It was a difficult thing to do. He knew he'd trained all of his sons well. He knew that none of them had any habits or anything else that was a concern when it came to doing the jobs. What worried him most of all was the fear of something happening to any of them. He'd seen Max in a hospital bed two years earlier, confined in the deep slumber of a coma. That had scared Mitchell, leaving him wishing during that time that he could trade places with Max rather than Max suffer from the gunshot wound he'd received.

As he thought about that time, Mitchell's sight naturally shifted to Max. Mitchell had wondered for a long time if Max would wake up in that hospital, or if he might leave them forever. With so much time having passed since then, sometimes it now seemed as though the shooting had never happened. Max was alive, he was awake, and he was as happy as he'd ever been.

Thinking about his sons' love lives, Mitchell had to hold back a smile. Yes, they were all good kids.

If Caroline had still been alive, she would have been just as proud of who they'd each become, as he was.

Quietly, he remained still and refocused on everything that each of his sons was saying. As far as he could tell, they'd planned it all as perfectly as any other job they'd ever done. There was no concern in handing the family business over to Vic's control. There was no concern at all.

After a long while of quiet conversation, questions, answers, and agreement, Mitchell saw all of his sons stand. When Vic turned and looked straight at him, Mitchell grinned. He knew where his son was at. He'd been in that same spot decades earlier, knowing that he was going to be responsible for continuing the family business and being responsible for the safety of other people. It was a bittersweet moment in time, feeling anxious about what might happen, while at the same time feeling incredibly proud to be the next Stonewarden to lead and continue the family's heritage.

"You're going to be fine, Vic," Mitchell reassured his oldest son. "If I didn't think you were ready for this, I wouldn't be sending you out as leader yet."

"I know," Vic said, nodding. "I'm okay," he continued before turning back to his brothers.

Between the five of them, they loaded up the vehicles with themselves and everything they'd need. It was going to be the start of a new phase of the Stonewarden legacy. Hopefully, it would go off without a glitch.

CHAPTER 3

Sitting back in the seat of the car that Vic was driving, Max thought about Christy - the woman he'd been seeing for months. The two of them had been taking their time to get to know one another, and he was enjoying it. Admittedly, in more recent times, he had been finding it more difficult to keep Christy at arm's length as far as sex went. Time and time again she'd let him know that she wanted it to happen, but Max feared he might hurt her if they rushed to it, so they'd waited.

With adrenaline running through his veins, he had to force himself to stop thinking about her. She knew nothing about his life in the family business. Everything about Christy was good. It was difficult to imagine that she could ever accept what Max was about to do that night, or on any of the many other nights when he'd helped to steal gems.

"What was that sigh for?" he heard Regan ask from the passenger seat in the front.

"Nothing I want to talk about right now," Max replied. At that moment, he could have easily engaged in conversation about his feelings about the family business while he was involved with someone. He knew that Regan had been seeing his girlfriend for years. Did she know about his criminal side of life? And what about Vic - his other brother in the car. Max had never heard Vic talk about any women in his life. Was he involved with anyone? Did *they* know what he did in his family time?

So many questions, he could have asked.

Instead, he shook his head in determination to push his questions aside. When they did a job, they each needed to fully focus. Usually it had never been a problem for Max. The women he'd previously spent time with, he'd seen so little of that it was never anything worth worrying about. Christy was the first woman he'd met who'd truly captured his attention and held it.

It took all of his willpower to switch off completely. In his head, he focused on the role he was about to play, and how everything was going to go. There was no room in his thoughts for anything else - or anyone.

"You two ready?" he heard Vic ask as the car slowed to a stop.

"Yep," said Max, looking at the backs of the heads of one brother and then the other.

"Yep," he heard Regan say.

"Let's do this then," Vic said.

The job was on.

CHAPTER 4

While Christy Jones traveled home from her job at the local police station, she was already calculating all that she'd need to do between getting home and heading out again. It was the night that she visited the homeless shelter each week to help with the service of meals. Although she knew that serving homeless people wasn't something that was for everyone, she absolutely loved it. It wasn't a chore for her. It also wasn't something that had ever made her feel uncomfortable. If anything, it had provided her with a feeling of being accepted when she'd previously felt like she couldn't fit in anywhere.

As she thought about her volunteer role at the center, her mind turned to another pleasant subject. Max Stonewarden had been spending a lot of time with her. Initially, she'd found it difficult to believe that a guy like him could be interested in a girl like her. He'd worked hard to help her believe that his intentions were real and not some build-up to an upcoming discomfort that her head tried to tell her was inevitable.

Max had put in the hours to help her feel comfortable with him. His efforts had paid off. When Christy now thought about their time together, her head was no longer so successful in making her believe it must be some kind of joke that he was spending time with her.

Over their time of getting to know one another, they'd gotten much closer than Christy had ever been to anyone. She'd opened up to him in ways that she'd never felt comfortable doing with anyone before. She'd also begun to get close to him physically. That was something she'd never done before either. At times when they kissed, she wanted to be closer to him in that way. At other times, she found it overwhelming that she wanted to be with him, but she couldn't bear the thought of him seeing her naked. Her body wasn't like other women's. She was short. She was round. She couldn't see past that, no matter how much Max tried to reassure her that he saw her as attractive.

As she entered her apartment, she contemplated a similar question that she'd asked herself many times before. Why was she so sure that she couldn't be loved? She suspected it was the basis of everything to do with how she'd always felt about herself, but where had that belief come from? There was nothing in her lifelong memory that she thought could have produced such a belief, but it had been there for as long as she could remember anything.

After assembling her early dinner, she sat down on her sofa and resolved not to think about the negative things she knew her mind liked to settle on. To help shift her focus, she thought about Max again. Every night for the previous few weeks, he'd had to spend time with his family. Why that was, Christy didn't know. He'd never provided an explanation, and she'd never asked for one. In her eyes, if he was spending that much time with his family, that was a great thing. It showed just how close the Stonewardens must be as a family unit. From her job at the police station, Christy could only appreciate families who believed in the importance of spending quality time together.

As much as she had no problem with Max spending each evening with his family, she had to admit that she was excited about him having said that he was on the last night of the lengthy nightly routine. Thinking about that made Christy smile. She didn't imagine herself to be a possessive person, and she certainly would never ask anyone to choose her over their family, but the two of them being able to spend evenings together would be nice. There were still so many things for them to explore.

Explore. It was a word that she'd not thought about too often in the past, but it was what she wanted to do with Max. She'd told him she was ready for them to move forward with sex, and she definitely was. While eating her meal, she thought about the times they'd gotten closer.

The first time she'd laid on top of Max, he'd encouraged her, and reassured her that she wasn't as heavy as she thought she was. She'd found it hard to let go of her concern about him being underneath her. Since then, they'd laid down together several times. Each time, it had been easier. Her body issues were never far from her thoughts, but she was at least slowly learning to relax and ignore them.

After eating her meal and taking time to get refreshed in the shower, she moved into her bedroom. Before dressing, she forced herself to stand in front of her mirror fully naked and look at herself. It was never easy. Was there anything attractive about her body? Not that she could see. She didn't think she'd ever truly like what she saw in her reflection, but she was beginning to at least accept it. That was a good start.

When her alarm went off to remind her that she was due to leave to go to the shelter, Christy laughed softly at herself. Standing around, looking at herself naked, was hardly accomplishing anything. She quickly dressed and left her apartment. Whatever lay ahead for her, or for her and Max, was unknown. Even so, she knew she was going through a period of change, and that was something to rejoice in.

Yes, there was much to look forward to.

CHAPTER 5

Once at the shelter for the homeless, Christy got straight to work in the kitchen. She wasn't a chef, but she was always happy to help the center out however she could, even if that meant the monotony of peeling dozens of carrots.

"How's that handsome young man of yours this week, Christy?" she heard an older woman, Teresa, ask.

"You haven't met him, Teresa," Christy said, chuckling. "How do you know he's handsome?"

"Of course he's handsome!" Teresa said with a mock look of shock on her face. "Why, no other kind of man deserves your kind heart."

"Thank you," Christy said, smiling. "Well, *I* think he's handsome. He did come in here one time, but you weren't here that night."

"No, but I heard all about it," said Teresa. "Oh yes, everyone said how nice he was. Is he treating you right?"

Christy took a moment to ask herself that question. Was Max treating her right? She'd spent so long thinking he was going to set her up only to hurt her that her initial view of him surprised her sometimes. Pondering the time they'd already spent together, she only had one answer to the question.

"Yes, he is lovely," she said, her mind pushing the silent question into her mind about whether that was true.

"Good girl," said Teresa. "Never settle for someone who doesn't deserve you! Now, can you start setting up the serving area for me? These will take only ten minutes to cook, and then we'll be ready to let the masses in."

Christy smiled and moved to do as she'd been asked to. After her work at the police station, often dealing with people who'd done varying degrees of crimes, there was something refreshing about being able to help out those in need at the shelter. They weren't all angels, of course. Plenty of people who lived on the streets had either been in prison or might be heading there, but there were equally those who Christy met at the shelter who she didn't believe had any bad in them. Bad luck, maybe, but not general *bad*.

When the doors opened, the usual line began to move inwards. Christy happily stood behind the row of bain-maries, chatting briefly with each person who wanted the food she was responsible for. It was a joy to her, seeing the smiles that came from her just asking how they were. The people she served had so little, but some of them were always so happy.

"I can see you're itching to get out there and chat, lass, so off you go," one of the leaders said to her once the initial rush at the food service area was complete.

Christy grinned. Among the crowd sitting at the tables were a lot of regulars who she'd spoken to many times. Slowly, she moved around, checking in with the people she'd gotten to know to see how they were doing. When she'd talked to them, she began to walk around the people she'd never met previously.

"Excuse me, Miss," a man said from behind her. When Christy turned toward the voice, she saw him looking at her, although not with a smile. "Can you sit and talk with me a while?"

Watching his face and hearing his tone, Christy

felt wary but put on her standard smile and crouched down beside him.

"Hi," she said. "I'm Christy. And you are?"

"Greg," the man said, holding out his hand. "Greg Winterburn."

Christy briefly held back from shaking his hand. Having worked at the police station for so many years, it was rare that she felt a strong unease with people. She may not have usually been confident inside of herself, but she'd grown used to having to work out how to liaise with some extreme members of society.

When she forced herself to shake his hand, she also forced herself to maintain the smile on her face.

"I'm pleased to meet you, Greg," she said before embarking on a short interaction of basic small talk. It was the first time that she'd felt so uneasy around anyone who'd passed through the shelter mealtimes when she'd been working.

After several minutes, she moved on to someone else, and the conversation was forgotten.

CHAPTER 6

At the end of the meal service, Christy was subjected to more teasing from Teresa. She didn't mind it. Since the subject was Max, she knew there were far worse things she could have been forced to embark on a conversation about.

"So, are you seeing your Romeo tonight?" the older woman asked.

"No, not tonight, Teresa," Christy replied. "He's got something on with his dad and brothers tonight."

"Oh! A family man! That's a great sign," Teresa said as she wiped down the last area of service bench. "A man who enjoys his family is a man who will be worthy of you, young lady."

"Hopefully," said Christy, for a moment feeling her usual sliver of doubt.

"I remember when I met my Tony..." Teresa began to say. It was a story Christy had heard many times before, but she never tired of listening to the romantic way that Teresa described the start of her lifelong relationship with her husband.

Christy was soon absorbed into the story. Now and then, some of the details changed, but she didn't mind. The thought of loving someone for a lifetime seemed like the stuff of fairytales. She saw examples of it being possible all around her. Believing that it could be something that she might experience herself wasn't as easy.

"Oh, but listen to me prattle on," Teresa said, breaking Christy out of her thoughts. "You must be getting home. Young ladies all need their beauty sleep, Christy! That is one of my secrets for having a long and enjoyable lifetime - sleep!"

Christy chuckled but nodded.

"Thanks, Teresa," she said. "I will get going now if you're sure you can finish up here without me?"

"I can," Teresa replied, grinning. "Off you go. Keep safe, and we'll see you next week."

Christy smiled again and nodded before grabbing her coat and preparing to leave. Walking out into the warm air, she felt good. It had been another enjoyable evening talking and listening to people who weren't as fortunate as she was. She often pondered that. She was young, but she had a good job and a roof over her head. How did people with far more life experience end up living on the streets with no job and no roof over their heads? Sometimes the people she spoke to shared their stories of the transition from a previously happy and well set-up life to where they currently were. She'd heard some tales that were sad. She'd also heard some that were horrific. What some people were able to go through and survive never ceased to amaze her.

"Hey, Little Lady," she heard a voice say from behind her when she was out on the street.

Feeling her body instantly grow alert and anxious, Christy kept her head forward as if she hadn't heard it. It was a pointless exercise. When she'd taken a few more steps, the voice revealed the face it belonged to. She recognized the man as one that she'd spoken to earlier - Greg Winterburn.

"Oh, hello," she said quietly while continuing to quicken her pace. "I'm sorry that I can't talk right now. I'm meeting someone, but I'll see you again at the shelter another time?"

She hoped that would give the man the hint that

she didn't want to speak to him. In the back of her mind, she suspected the effort might be futile.

"Meeting someone?" Greg asked as he persisted in walking alongside her. "Or walking to the bus stop?"

On hearing his question, Christy felt her nervousness increase. Did he know that was where she was going? If so, did that mean that he'd been watching her for some time?

"Please," she said, trying with all her might to hold onto hope that he was just being friendly and didn't have any other intentions. "I … I … *please* don't walk with me."

"You shouldn't be out here alone," Greg said. "Anything could happen."

Christy's anxiety and nervousness quickly escalated into fear. Looking ahead of her, she hoped she would see someone - anyone - but it was too late at night. There was nobody to be seen. Without speaking again, she began to walk faster. It wasn't easy. She was overweight, and she was unfit. At that moment, she wished more than ever before that she'd prioritized exercise and health. If for no other reason, it would have made it much easier to get away from the very scenario that she'd found herself in.

"Thank you," she said, trying to display a far more relaxed display of calm than she felt. "But, really, I am fine. See you at the shelter next week?"

As she continued to walk, for a moment it seemed as though Greg had stopped. It wasn't a long moment at all.

"I'll at least walk you to the bus stop," he said, catching up to her easily while striding at a walking pace faster than Christy could manage. "Your bus isn't for… seventeen minutes. I hate to think that you're out here all alone."

Christy felt panic begin to set in. He knew that she was catching a bus, and he knew *which* bus she was catching. Did that mean that he knew where she lived too? The thought was a horrific one. She knew many people at the shelter had dark pasts, and some had dark presents. Despite that truth, she'd never before felt like she was a target of any of them.

Resolved that she probably wouldn't be able to persuade him to leave her alone, Christy walked as fast as she could. She wouldn't be able to shake him off, but at least she could remain in the light so that if any cars went by, she was visible. She said nothing more to him but remained aware that he was right there, close behind her.

When she finally reached the bus stop, she felt a little relieved. More than one bus went past it. Hopefully, that meant there might be more witnesses if anything happened to her. While she hated the thought of something 'happening to her', she worked in the local police station. She read reports of abuse and violence every day in her job. She'd also read a fair few reports centered around murders. The one thing she'd always promised herself was that if she was in a dark situation, she had to at least make sure she wasn't taken away anywhere. At times, she'd laughed at herself for considering something bad might happen to her. As she moved to stand directly under the street lamp at the bus stop, she was thankful she'd read as much as she had in her job.

"Thank you for walking with me," she said as the man she was beginning to fear stood beside her. "I'm fine now."

"Fine?" Greg asked, his tone dropping the friendly façade it had held till then. "You're a young woman out here in the dark of night all alone. You're not fine," he continued as he took yet another step closer to her. "I'm sure you get lots of offers from boys, but I bet you'd like a man, huh?"

As Christy felt his hand on her arm, she focused on the same thought she'd had earlier. Whatever happened, she did not want to move from directly under the street lamp. A bus would come along, and there would be at least one person on it who could help her if need be. If she moved into the darkness, her only chance of being safe, if the man who'd grabbed her intended to hurt her, would be gone.

"Stop!" she said as she tried to move her arm out of his grasp. It was useless. "What are you doing? Why are you grabbing me?"

Hearing him laugh as his grip tightened pushed Christy over the edge from being scared to being angry. She'd put up with crap from guys almost all of her life. At school, they'd set her up only to make a fool out of her. She'd endured teasing and humiliation. She'd endured guys pretending to like her, only to turn out to be nasty. At that moment, as the man beside her gripped her arm as tightly as he had, she felt a very long overdue rage surface. Unfortunately, it was at the same time that Greg Winterburn pulled a knife from his jacket pocket.

"Come with me," he said. "You know you want to."

As Christy felt his hand attempt to pull her by her arm, she knew she'd reached a limit of what she'd put up with. A year or two earlier and she would have been a blithering mess in her current situation. The time that she'd spent with Max Stonewarden had changed her. Had he fully succeeded in making her think more about her value as a human being? No. But he had helped her to gain more self-confidence than she'd ever had before.

Feeling her frustrations pull together into one

rage, she successfully pulled her arm from Greg's grasp. As she did, the mutual turning of their bodies resulted in the knife in his hand making contact with her side.

The sharpness of the blade sinking in made Christy look down in surprise. It was little time before the red of her blood began to soak through the sweater she had on. Another slice of time made her feel weak, unable to stand.

As she lowered to the ground, she could feel her awareness begin to fade away. Greg Winterburn running into the darkness was the last thing she saw.

CHAPTER 7

When the boys had left the Stonewarden family home, Mitchell had remained sitting where he had been during their final planning. He knew the expected time for the boys to finish the job. When it was over, he expected Max, Fitz, and Vic to all return to the family home. James would be going straight to his apartment. Regan would be going to see his girlfriend at her apartment. Plans were expected. That didn't mean they always were followed.

Glancing at his watch, he could see that it was half an hour past the time that Vic had guessed they'd be done by. It made Mitchell nervous. Not only were the boys not home, but they'd also not made any contact to indicate something was wrong.

To divert his thoughts and concerns, he turned on the TV. In his opinion, it was a mindless box that sat in the corner of the living room. Throughout his lifetime, he'd only ever turned it on when they'd done a job and he wanted to see if anything about it was on the news. At all other times, he was happy to enjoy the peace of his home or the happy sound of any of his kids.

As the late news began, he monitored it for any report about a jewelry burglary. There was none. That was a relief. If anything happened to any of his kids…

"We're home," he heard Max say as the front door opened.

Seeing Vic and Max both enter the living room, Mitchell expected one more son to walk in.

"Fitz isn't with us," Vic said. "Said he had

things to do and somewhere to go."

Mitchell shook his head but said nothing in response to the statement. Where his youngest son could have gone at such a time of night, he didn't know. What he did know was that there was no point in asking Fitz or anyone else about it. Fitz lived by his own rules when he wasn't working a family job. Mitchell had long ago accepted that. He worried about it, but he accepted it.

"All okay?" Mitchell asked Vic and saw him nod.

"Yep, no problem at all," Vic replied, grinning. He couldn't deny that having watched his brothers all do their part in the job while following his lead and instruction had been highly invigorating once it had begun. Any previous feelings of anxiety that he'd had, he'd forgotten once the job was underway. "Here."

Mitchell stood and walked to the coffee table to see the contents of what the boys had gathered. He wasn't a jewelry expert, but he knew enough to be able to see that they'd done well.

"What do we do now?" Vic asked, eager to continue the next part of his training.

Mitchell smiled at him. Until that night, he'd been the only one to facilitate the next stage in the processing of the gems. It was exciting for him to be embarking on introducing Vic to the routines that followed.

"Now we take these to be processed," he said as he pointed at the jewelry.

"Well, I'm going to bed - unless you need me for anything else?" asked Max.

"No," his father replied.

"Thanks, Max," Vic added before seeing his younger brother smile and then walk out. When he was alone with his father, he turned to face him again.

"Do we do this now, or…"

"It's late," Mitchell said. "I normally do take these as soon as a job is finished, but if you need to get home…"

"No, I … I'd rather keep doing things the way they've always been done," said Vic. "If it's normal to do whatever you do with these now, I'm happy to do that."

"Alright," said Mitchell, nodding. "Gather those up, and let's go see Big John."

"Big John?" Vic asked. "Is that his real name?"

Mitchell chuckled but nodded again.

"Yep," he said. "When you see him, you'll see why."

Once settled into the car, Vic could still feel his heart pounding from the excitement of the evening. In his hand, he held his phone, recording onto a map the route that his father was taking them on. One day his father wouldn't be by his side at all for jobs. As sad as that thought was, Vic wanted to be fully prepared and able to continue the Stonewarden legacy with pride and confidence when that day came.

"How are you feeling?" his father asked as if sensing Vic's mood.

"I feel …great!" Vic exclaimed. Turning to look at his father, he could see the smile that he knew was one of happiness. "Are you sure you're ready to pass over the organizing of jobs, Dad? Was it … *strange* … staying home tonight?"

"Yeah, it was," said Mitchell. "But I'm not getting any younger, Vic. Whatever life I have left, I want to enjoy it more, and I know you've been itching to be in charge for a while. You're more than ready, and I'm happy with you stepping up."

"Thanks," Vic said quietly as he looked out the window. They'd driven away from the city, resulting in just black outside. Although a random light here and there indicated the odd house now and then, Vic was aware of how remote they were getting. He'd initially not understood his father's suggestion to record the location and route to get there. With the outside being as dark as it was, the request made sense. "Where is this place?"

"Not far now," Mitchell replied.

"And this guy will still be up?" asked Vic.

"Yep, Big John is always informed ahead of time when approximately we'll - *you'll* - be done," said Mitchell. "For as long as he's doing this job, he'll be at the ready for you to drop the takings to him as soon as you're done."

"As long as he's doing this job?" Vic asked. "Is he expected to not be doing it at some point?"

"Big John's a lot older than me," Mitchell said. "He might or might not want to retire, but at some point soon, someone else is going to have to be trained to do his job, otherwise there's possibly going to be a lapse in time when there's nobody to do the processing." He turned and looked at his son. "This is something you might need to start thinking about soon, Vic. Someone's going to have to be chosen to do the job that Big John does."

"Okay," Vic said, nodding. He had no idea what the job entailed, let alone who could do it.

"Don't worry about it tonight," Mitchell said, smiling. "Right now, just focus on what you're about to see."

Vic looked at his father. The words just spoken made it seem like they were going to see something amazing. It was difficult to imagine what that could possibly be in the middle of nowhere.

"And here we are," Mitchell said as he pulled into a driveway.

As Vic looked forward, he could see a large old farmhouse with a dim light on over the porch entranceway. There was nothing spectacular that he could see about the house itself. He turned and looked at his father as if to ask the silent question about what was so special about where they'd stopped. His father only smiled at him and indicated they get out.

With the small package of jewelry secured in his jacket pocket, Vic watched as the front door of the home opened and a large man walked out. The grin he gave as he greeted Mitchell was one of true joy.

"And this is Vic, all grown up!" Big John said as he turned to face Vic with his hand outstretched. "Last time I saw you, you were only this high. You've grown a bit!" he continued, chuckling. "But come inside, where it's warm."

After ushering them through the large open foyer and into a smaller living area, Big John turned to face them.

"Now, what have you gathered tonight?" he asked, looking from Mitchell to Vic.

Vic glanced at his father and received a nod before he pulled the small parcel out of his jacket pocket. He watched as Big John carefully took the parcel and opened it slowly, his eyes lighting up at what he saw inside.

"This … this is a fine haul," Big John said. "Shouldn't take more than four days for me to do this lot."

"Big John, I know it's late, but would you mind showing Vic your secret hideaway?" Mitchell asked, grinning.

Big John chuckled but nodded.

"It is a world of wonder and mystery, Vic," he teased. "Would you like to see it?"

"Yes?" Vic asked, feeling like he was engaging

in some kind of joke that only the other two people in the room were aware of.

"Come this way," Big John said.

After they walked through the large kitchen, Vic stood in awe as he saw Big John manipulate controls hidden inside the large walk-in pantry. Before his eyes, a space opened up that would never be visible to the average person, no matter how well they searched the house.

Vic remained quiet as he followed Big John and his father down a dark staircase. When a light was switched on, Vic was beyond surprised. He'd just walked through a very standard, very old farmhouse. The room he was standing in was harsh white with the glossiness of looking brand new. However it was used, it was modern, it was well-structured, and it was almost clinical. It also had a well set-up wall of monitors that showed camera feeds from all angles around and inside the upper level of the home.

"You like?" Big John asked Vic, grinning at the look of surprise on his face. "This, Vic, is where the magic happens. Down here, I take jewelry such as this," he said, laying the stolen items out carefully on a green felt pad inside a wide glass case that was positioned at the perfect height for standing and working at. "And I transform it into pieces such as this," he continued as he redirected Vic's attention to another workbench and case a short distance away.

Vic followed Big John and looked at the finished products. He'd been stealing jewelry for long enough to be able to identify quality products from products that weren't real, but he didn't know about value beyond that.

"You make them unidentifiable?" Vic asked.

"Yes, but that isn't all these are," Big John said as he pointed at the newly formed pieces. "The gems that come out of the original pieces each have their own unique identifying marks, so I make sure that they are reduced down enough so that those natural signatures are no longer visible. The more important aspect of doing this, however, is that in this form - something smaller and more common-looking - these are easier to sell. The jewelry you bring to me is mostly larger, more expensive items that only the elite of society can afford to buy. They buy it, and they keep it, often not wearing it or truly appreciating it. But these pieces - what I create - these pieces are made to be affordable and loved by average people who will appreciate and look after them."

"But their value…" Vic began to ask.

"I see your confusion," Big John said. "You wonder if small pieces like this, purchased by average people, can possibly add up to the same value as the larger, more exclusive pieces they come from."

"Yes," Vic said, nodding.

"It is a good question, but not one that is easy to answer," said Big John. "The elite pieces of jewelry in the world are usually purchased at exceptional prices, it is true, but like anything, the value is only dictated by what someone will pay for it."

"But everything has a price tag," said Vic.

"It does, but if you put a high price on something and it never sells, is it truly worth the price you have given it? Is the worth of something what someone says it is worth, or what someone is willing to pay for it?"

"Hmm," Vic mumbled, intrigued.

"To answer the question, it would always be possible that if we were to try and sell these items in their original form, we might find a buyer who will pay a premium price, but who, then, are we helping by stealing the piece to begin with? With what we do, we can take the original items, transform them into pieces that people can afford and will treasure, and we can then take our proceeds to use to help others in need," Big John said. "All of the jewelry that we have ever transformed into new pieces has been sold."

"All of it?" asked Vic. "Every piece?"

"Every piece," Big John confirmed, nodding.

"Who do you sell it to?"

"*I* don't sell it to anyone," Big John said, chuckling. "I am but one link in a very long chain, Vic. My job is purely to transform the few of those," he said, pointing at the newly acquired pieces. "Into many of those," he continued, pointing at already transformed pieces.

"Then who…?" Vic began to ask his father.

"Beyond this is the responsibility of another member of the family, Vic," said Mitchell. "Right now, this is the first part that you need to be aware of. There's plenty of time for you to learn what happens after this point of the process."

Vic nodded. He was eager to learn and know more, but respected his father's ways of doing things. They were the ways that had been done for generations, as far as he was aware. He could wait and learn at whatever pace his father set.

"So, if I'm in the position that you've been in all these years, do I need to come back and get these new pieces?" he asked.

"No," Big John replied. "You bring the acquisitions to me as soon as you can after each job. From there, I'll do my bit, and the process will carry on from here. Every piece of the puzzle is kept separate, even though we are all in it together, if that makes sense."

Vic nodded even though he didn't quite understand.

"Well, we won't keep you up any longer, Big John," Mitchell said and saw Big John laugh.

"I hardly ever sleep these days, Mitchell," Big John said. "Old age, you know. Which brings me to one thing we shall need to discuss sometime soon. You know I love doing this, but…"

"But it's time for someone new to be taught your skill?" Mitchell asked, amused by the coincidence that he'd just had a similar conversation with Vic in the car.

"Yes," Big John replied. "It is something that takes time to learn and master. Someone with youth on their side who would like to work in a role like this would be most suitable. It's not hard work physically, but it takes patience and the ability to focus."

"I'll - *we'll* - get onto finding someone suitable for you to train as soon as possible," Mitchell said.

Big John nodded and led them out of the basement and up through the old kitchen again.

"Come and see me next week so we can discuss how to work towards training and changeover," he said to both men at the front door. "Don't get me wrong. I'll be alive for another century yet, I have no doubt, but better to be ready…"

Mitchell chuckled and shook his hand before saying goodbye.

"Nothing to worry about there, then," Vic said to his father when they started their journey back to the city.

"No, Big John is easy going, and flexible too," said Mitchell. "There have been times when he's come to wherever I've been with the gems, if I haven't been able to get to him. He's a valued member of our entire team."

"But, Dad, I don't know who our entire team *is*," said Vic. "I thought it was just us - you and us kids. I didn't know there were more people out there doing other stuff as well."

"I know," Mitchell said. "There are a lot of people who contribute to our family legacy. It took time for me to understand how it all worked and who was involved. It won't take you as long to gain an understanding of it all. I'll work through it all much better and faster than my father did with me."

"I never met your father," said Vic. "You don't talk about your parents."

Mitchell turned his head and looked at his son. It was rare for Vic to say much at all, except for the serious nature of the jobs they did.

"No, I hardly ever think about them now," said Mitchell. "My mother was kind and loving. My father wasn't. But he was the one who forced me into the military, and for that, I am grateful. It made me grow up."

Vic nodded but didn't have any reply. In the back of his mind, he remembered his promise to Hayley that he'd message her when the job was done. He hadn't. Looking at his watch, he didn't want to risk waking her if he messaged her, but he had made a promise, and the journey back to the city would take some time.

Pulling out his phone, he typed the quickest and briefest message that he could, in case she was worried:

'Be home soon.'

Putting away his phone, he felt a familiar sadness about having an amazing partner that nobody else in his family knew, or had even heard of.

CHAPTER 8

When Max woke up the following morning, his thoughts immediately went to his internal conflict about the job that he did, and the feelings he had for Christy. He hated lying to her about his family business, even if it was only lying by omission.

The time they'd spent together hadn't been defined by any particular label, but he believed that his feelings for her were real. Maybe they were driven by an internal need to be closer to her physically. Would he still feel the same way about her if they crossed that line and finally had sex? He hoped so, but he conceded that things might change once they ventured into that unknown. Still, it was nice to have watched her open up and slowly grow more comfortable in her own skin. When he'd first met Christy, her ongoing self-loathing had been evident. He was glad to have witnessed the change in her over the time that he'd known her.

Picking up his phone, he noted the time. It was too early to message her, but he would definitely do so a little later. For a long while, he'd considered introducing her to at least some members of his family. The first one would have to be Charlie. She was the sibling that Max was closest to. He didn't doubt that by introducing her to Christy, he would be teased by Charlie for a long time afterward, but it would be worth it. Charlie was chilled, and Max had no doubt she would accept Christy as easily as he had.

Suddenly eager to get on with the day and go spend some time with his sister, he jumped out of bed.

He'd be respectful of others' need for sleep, but he had to move. He took his time to shower, dress, and head down to the kitchen to find food before he picked up his phone again.

'You home and up for a visitor today?' he messaged his sister.

'Yeah, of course,' Charlie replied a few minutes later.

Max smiled to himself.

"That's quite a grin for so early in the morning," he heard his father, Mitchell, say as he entered the kitchen. "What's going on with you?"

"Nothing much," Max replied. While he knew he could talk to his father about anything, he didn't feel the need to. "Just sorting out my day."

"Hmm," Mitchell replied, grinning but not attempting to get anything more out of his son. His sons had done their first job without him the night before. They'd done the job, and there had been no hiccups. He was relieved, happy, and as proud as any parent could be.

When Mitchell had left the kitchen, coffee in hand, Max picked up his phone again.

'I'd like to take you to meet Charlie today,' he typed in a message to Christy. Getting no reply for a couple of minutes, he continued, assuming she was still asleep. *'Let me know what you think.'*

He kept the screen on for another couple of minutes, just in case she replied. When no reply came, he happily turned it off and got on with enjoying his breakfast.

CHAPTER 9

As the hours passed and he'd still heard nothing from Christy, Max began to worry. She had her own life, of course, and she was busy in it. Even so, she was usually pretty quick to get back to him, even if just to say she was busy and she'd message fully later. He didn't know if he should be worried or not, but the long delay in her response did seem a little out of character for her.

"You okay?" his father asked when Max entered the living room and didn't hide his concern. "What's happened?"

"Not sure," Max said, glancing at his phone again. "I messaged Christy this morning, and she hasn't replied."

"Is that a concern?" Mitchell asked.

"I don't know," said Max. "I mean, she's probably at work. Maybe something's come up there."

"Does she usually message you when she's working?" asked his father.

"Yeah, when she has a break," Max said as he glanced at his watch. "And she would normally have had a break by now."

"Is this the young woman you were gushing over on the phone ages ago? The one from the cop shop?" Mitchell asked, remembering very well the humorous silkiness of his son's voice that day.

"Yeah," Max replied.

"You've been seeing her all this time?"

"Yes! Geez, Dad," Max said, feeling his father's attempt to keep things lighthearted.

"If you're worried about her, call her at work," Mitchell said when he noticed just how serious his son looked. "Can't be too hard to find the number for the local police station. Call and make sure that she's okay."

"Yeah … but what if she just doesn't want to talk to me or something?" asked Max, his concern changing to a rare instance of self-doubt.

Mitchell studied his son's face. It wasn't usual for any of his sons to sound unconfident. For kids who'd grown up in the situation they had, they all had been remarkably successful when it came to the opposite sex.

"Well, if that's the case, you'll just have to accept it, but I can see that you're worried about her, so ring them and ask, or go to the cop shop and see her," said Mitchell. "At least then you'll know she's okay. If she has any reason for not wanting to talk to you, it's still best that you make sure she is alright if her not replying is out of character for her."

"Yeah, okay," said Max. "I'm not going to call them, though. I'll just head over. She works on the front desk. I'll just say a quick hi and make sure she is okay."

Without waiting to hear any more words from his father, Max grabbed his car keys and swiftly went out to his Mustang. The gruntiness of the engine starting usually gave him something to smile about. At that moment, he didn't even notice it. His mind was on something else, and his concern was growing by the minute.

All the way from his home to the police station, he tried to think of any reason that Christy might not want to speak to him. He knew she'd been talking about the two of them having sex, and he'd tried to avoid that situation. Had that affected her more than she'd let on? He knew that she was well experienced in using anything as a reason to dislike herself. Maybe she hadn't believed him when he'd told her that he was attracted to her and did want to have sex with her, just not yet. Maybe she'd reached a point where she'd waited long enough and didn't want to wait any longer for him. Maybe…

As the Mustang purred along, Max's mind remained active. It was difficult to believe that Christy might have decided she didn't want to know him anymore. Difficult, but not impossible.

Considering her walking away from him, Max felt sad. He'd respect her decision, but he wouldn't like it.

CHAPTER 10

"Hey," Max said as he approached the front desk and saw Christy's older workmate, Sandra, sitting behind it. "Is Christy here?

"Oh, no," Sandra said, standing and looking at him with a look of seriousness on her face.

Max was startled. Whenever he'd gone in to see Christy at her work, Sandra had always teased them, keeping a smile on her face. At that moment, her face wasn't smiling.

"What?" Max asked. "Is she upset with me? She hasn't replied to my messages…"

"Max, Christy was attacked last night," Sandra said. "Nobody told you?"

"No. Nobody would know…" he started to say before focusing on the word she'd used. "Attacked?" he asked and saw Sandra nod in confirmation. "What … what do you mean?"

"She … she was near the shelter she serves meals at each week, and a man from there attacked her," Sandra went on to say.

"But … but … is she…" Max started to ask as he felt himself grow a little faint. He'd experienced his mother dying. He didn't want to have to face the feelings associated with death and grief again. Not yet anyway.

"She's alive," Sandra finally said, smiling sadly. "She's at the hospital in intensive care, but she's alive."

Max didn't reply in any way, instead turning and running out the door. He wasted no time in starting the engine of his car and making sure he got to the hospital as quickly as he could.

Running through the large sliding glass doors at the front entrance, he was briefly reminded of the months that he'd spent in the building after the shooting. The thought of it made him shudder, but he pushed himself forward.

Following the signs to the intensive care unit, he swiftly found the information he needed and made his way to the room where Christy was.

"Max?" Christy asked when she opened her eyes and saw him tentatively entering.

"Hey," Max said as he walked to her bedside. "Sandra just told me you were here. Are you okay?" he asked. "I guess not, since you're in a hospital…"

As Christy heard him start to sound flustered, she giggled softly through the haziness she felt in her head. Hearing Max Stonewarden sound anything but confident and well-spoken was something she hadn't experienced before.

"I'm okay," she reassured him. "Well, I will be, the doctor has said. Just a little nick in my side, but they say it'll only be a week or two, and I'll be right as rain. I'm sorry I didn't message you. I didn't think…"

"That's okay. I'm just glad you're okay-*ish*. But what happened? How…?" Max began to ask. "Did the cops catch whoever did this to you?"

"Oh, it was … it was someone from the shelter, Max," Christy said, suspecting he wouldn't take the news well. "But … well, some of those people aren't nice, but most are. The police told me they have him in custody, so he's off the street now. Just a stroke of bad luck really. He could have followed anyone after work…"

"He *followed* you?" Max asked and saw her nod. "Christy, I never want to tell you what to do, but will you please let me take you there and pick you up from now on when you go?"

"Oh…" Christy said as she began to object. When she took a moment longer to consider how much worse things could have gone the night before, she nodded. "Okay. I might not go for a while now, though. Maybe it's time for a break."

Max nodded but didn't say anything. He knew she loved working at the shelter each week. If she was talking about having a break from it, she must have been truly freaked out. He didn't want to prolong her thoughts about that. As much as he wanted to ask questions about who the guy was and what was happening about his actions, he changed the subject instead.

"Well, when you're out of here, I'm gonna take you to meet Charlie … if you want to," he said quietly.

"Yeah, of course," said Christy. "I mean, if you want…"

"I want!" Max said, grinning. "I talked to Charlie this morning and was going to surprise you by taking you out there today. Now you'll have something to look forward to when you get out of here."

Christy smiled at him. Although she felt bad that she hadn't contacted him when she'd woken in the hospital, she knew the reason for that was her insecurity. She hadn't thought he'd be worried or even interested in knowing. That realization saddened her. She'd thought she'd come a long way in growing her self-confidence since he'd come into her life. Still, on occasion, she realized just how far she still had to go in making permanent changes to her opinion and thinking about herself.

"Thank you," she said quietly.

Max studied her face for a long time before he couldn't hold back anymore from kissing her. After leaning forwards and placing his lips on hers, he pulled back and looked into her eyes to see if that was okay.

"That makes me feel better," Christy said. "I might need some more," she added, feeling bold.

Max chuckled but happily did as he'd been instructed to do. As his lips caressed hers, he had an alarming thought that although she seemed fine in spirits, she had been attacked. Whatever the outcome was from that, it could have been far worse. Considering that left Max surprisingly emotional.

When Christy saw him pull back a second time, she saw in his eyes the telltale signs of tears being held back.

"What is it?" she asked as she reached up and caressed his face.

"You mean so much to me," Max admitted as he took her hand in his and kissed her palm. "Please be careful in whatever you do."

Christy smiled sadly at him as she reached around and gently pulled his head close again. When she'd woken, she hadn't thought he needed to be bothered by knowing what had happened to her. Being so close to him again, and seeing how emotional he was, she chose to believe that his feelings for her might just be as real as hers were for him.

"I know," she finally replied. "Yeah, it was silly for me to be walking around by myself at night, but usually it seems safe. I've been doing it for a long time now and nothing's happened before, but I do like the idea of keeping a bit safer in the future. I ... I was really scared when I heard him behind me."

Max nodded and squeezed her hand, holding back from asking anything. She'd taken a long time to open up to him about any of her real feelings. He'd learned not to push too hard. In her own time, if she needed to talk about anything, she would.

"I'm just glad that you're safe now," he said quietly before placing his lips on hers again. If there was nothing else he could do for her at that moment, he could keep reminding her that he valued who she was, and he thought she was amazing.

Christy smiled and pushed thoughts of the event aside in her mind. It would haunt her enough in the future when she had to play whatever role she needed to with the police investigation into what had happened. For the moment, she could relax. Close to her, kissing her, was a man who was slowly succeeding in encouraging her to feel good about herself. He didn't need to be at the hospital. He didn't need to have gone to her work earlier that morning to check that she was alright. He'd done those things purely because he'd wanted to. That said a lot.

"I really get to meet your sister?" she asked him in a teasing tone.

"Yeah, I really want that," Max said as he grinned and nodded. "I want you to meet all of my family, but Charlie's cool. I think you guys will get on well."

Christy smiled and felt tears threaten. Over a long period, knowing Max Stonewarden had been helping to chip away at her insecurities. She'd never expected to have any guy want to spend time with her in any way other than to tease her or make a fool out of her. On occasion, those fears still appeared in her mind, but her heart was slowly beating them down. It was a slow process. She knew that.

"Are you crying?" Max asked when he saw her eyes begin to glisten. "Did I say something wrong? You don't have to meet..."

"No!" Christy said with passion in her voice. "No, Max, I want to. I just … I … this is all new for me, that's all."

"I know," said Max. "It's new for me too. But don't worry about anything right now. You have to get better and be released from here first. After that, you can decide if you want to meet my family or not. For now, you just gotta focus on you."

Christy nodded and smiled again as she let her body relax.

"Will you stay for a while?" she asked as she looked at him through eyelids that were growing heavier.

"Yeah, I'm not going anywhere for now," said Max. "Get some sleep. I'll still be here when you wake next."

As odd as it felt to let herself fall asleep in front of him - in front of any guy - Christy didn't try and stop it from happening. She felt exhausted, and she wanted to get better. The sooner her body could heal, the sooner she could get back to knowing Max more, spending time with him, and meeting his sister. Also in their future might be the possibility of them getting closer physically. She hadn't been body-ready for that before. As she drifted off to sleep, she knew that she finally was.

CHAPTER 11

After ten days in the hospital, Christy was allowed to go home. Another week after that, she felt fully recovered. Inside of her apartment, Max had spent a lot of time with her during her recovery, fussing about in a way that had left her smiling a lot of the time, and giggling a lot more. He hadn't stayed over during the hours that she'd slept, but he'd made sure he was close by during almost all of the daylight hours. If there had been any doubt about his sincerity before Christy had been hurt, she knew it had completely melted away during the time they'd been in such close vicinity for so many hours each day. If Max Stonewarden was going to be like others, setting her up only to then humiliate her in some way, it was a hugely substantial prank. There was no piece of Christy that could allow for that to be the case.

"Hey, hey!" Max said when she opened the door to him the first morning that she'd woken feeling completely healed.

Christy smiled and stood aside to allow him access. Before he walked past her, she saw him halt in his steps, look at her lips in a way that she'd grown very used to, and then move close to her and kiss her with a passion that Christy was still eager to explore further. She happily wrapped her arms around him and held him close while indulging in his tongue playing with hers.

"Hmm," Max said, grinning as he pulled away. "You're alert this morning," he added with a small giggle.

"Hmm!" Christy said as she closed the door and followed him into her kitchen.

"Coffee?" she heard Max ask as she watched him already grabbing her cup and a cup for himself and then proceed to fill and turn on the kettle.

"Yep," Christy said as she chuckled to herself at just how at home the gorgeous man in front of her seemed to have made himself in her apartment.

While waiting for the water to boil, Max moved to where she stood and once again pulled her close. It was getting harder to keep the brakes on when it came to sex, but her body having needed time to heal had provided a firm reason why they couldn't get too carried away with their kissing. He was glad they'd had that time so he could care for her in other ways while keeping his desires in check. He didn't want to hurt her, but he couldn't deny that he was more than ready to move past any fears about that and share with her what they both wanted.

"Would you like to come with me to see Charlie today?" Max said as he pulled away to refocus on coffee-making. Not hearing a reply for a long moment, he looked up at Christy. "If you don't want to, that's okay, Christy."

"No!" Christy said. "No, if you…"

"Don't you say if I want to," Max said, pointing at her and laughing softly. "I asked you, which means I want to."

Christy giggled as she relaxed and nodded.

"Okay, then," she said. "Yes, I would like to go with you to meet your sister today."

She watched as she saw him grin. She felt nervous about showing herself to his family. She'd only just accepted that maybe he did like her as much as he kept saying he did. That didn't mean that other people would accept her as someone he should be with.

"Good," Max said as he handed her a cup. "Then drink this while you tell me about the dreams you had last night."

Christy grinned, nodded, and followed him to the sofa. What would be, would be, and that was quite okay.

CHAPTER 12

"Wow," Christy said when she saw where Max was driving her to. "Your sister lives here?" she asked as they moved up the long winding driveway, and a selection of buildings appeared in her view.

Max grinned as he turned and looked at her.

"Yeah," he said. "She doesn't own it. She and her husband, Ash, work and live here with an elderly couple - Tom and Molly," he continued as he placed a hand on Christy's knee. "Don't worry. They're all down to earth and friendly."

Christy smiled at him, reveling in the feeling of warmth that came from him touching her. There was nothing sexual about his touch, but she did feel sexual. She swiftly pushed that thought out of her mind.

When the Mustang's engine was turned off, Christy felt her anxiety kick in.

"You okay?" Max checked, sensing her mood change.

"Yes," Christy replied, nodding in determination to just get on with facing whatever was to come.

After exiting the Mustang, feeling Max's hand reach out and enclose hers was enough to at least help with Christy's anxiety about the situation she was embarking upon. She remained quiet as he led her to the front door.

"Hey, Ash," Max greeted Charlie's husband when it opened. "Is Charlie around?"

"Yeah, she's in the front room," Ash said, ushering the guests inside. "Come through."

When Charlie saw her brother walk in with a woman beside him, she was surprised but pleasantly so.

"Oh! Hello!" Charlie said, jumping up to pass her daughter to Max and then turn to the young woman.

"Charlie, Ash, this is Christy," Max finally said. "And this, Christy, is my niece, Caroline," he continued as he smiled and laughed at the infant reaching out to grab his nose.

Christy smiled at the two new adults in the room before turning her attention to Max holding the baby. She hadn't before thought about how he might be as a father. As she watched him giggling while he showed care in the way he held Caroline, Christy was pleased. She hadn't thought about having kids. She guessed it was still nice to know if a man looked like he would be a good dad.

"Sit down and relax, Christy," Charlie said to the woman, sensing her nervousness. "I must say, my brother talks about you quite a lot."

"Charlie!" Max exclaimed with affection.

"What?" Charlie asked with an innocent look and smile on her face. "I only said the truth!"

"That's not the point!" Max said, making both women laugh.

"I've got to go and help Tom with the donkeys," Ash said, standing up. "Do you want me to put her down?" he asked, glancing at Max holding the baby. The sight always made Ash smile.

"No, she's fine here," Charlie said before Ash leaned down and kissed her. "I'll give her another half hour and then put her down."

Christy watched the interaction between Max's sister and her husband. It was nice to see how they related to one another, both showing easy-going humor and love toward one another. She could only guess that it meant that Max and Charlie had both grown up witnessing love between their parents.

"Do you want a hand, Ash?" Max asked, surprising everyone in the room.

"Umm … okay," Ash replied.

"You only just got here!" Charlie said.

Max grinned at her as he handed Caroline to her.

"Yep," he said before turning to Christy and kissing her gently. "I'll be back soon."

When the men had left the two young women alone, Christy felt apprehension once again begin to sneak up on her.

"My brother doesn't do things without a reason, as I'm sure you know by now," Charlie said to the woman who looked uneasy. "He must want you and I to talk about something," she added, grinning.

"Oh!" Christy said, relaxing. "Do you think so?"

"I have no idea," Charlie said, chuckling. "But I am glad that he's brought you out here today. He's been talking about you for so long. It's something I'm really not used to."

"Oh?" Christy asked, feeling quite out of her depth.

"I can honestly say that I've never met any girl that Max has been involved with before, Christy," said Charlie. "In fact, I'm not sure I've ever seen him involved with anyone, the way that he is with you."

Christy smiled but said nothing, feeling her cheeks betray her nervousness at the situation.

"Sorry, I'm making you uncomfortable," Charlie said when she noticed Christy's discomfort. "No more talk of my brother! Tell me about you."

In Christy's mind, that was an even worse

subject, but she rose to the challenge. She couldn't - wouldn't - go on forever being afraid to interact with people and open up to them. Before her was a perfectly good situation where she could let herself speak and not be embarrassed by anything she wanted to say.

So she did.

CHAPTER 13

"Are you gonna tell me what's really going on, Max?" Ash asked when the two of them had left the house. "I mean, I appreciate the offer of help, but … this isn't normal."

"Yeah, sorry," Max said to his brother-in-law. "Actually, I wanted to talk to you."

"About?" asked Ash.

"About … you accepting our family when you accepted Charlie," said Max.

Ash nodded. Of course that was what would be on Max's mind. Inside the ranch house was a woman who'd captured his attention but didn't know about the Stonewardens. Ash wasn't surprised that it was him who'd been sought out to ask the question to.

"I love your sister, Max," he said.

"I know, but lots of people walk away from … that … because the situation isn't right," Max said.

"True, but me and Charlie aren't in the same situation as you'll be with whoever you're with," said Ash. "She didn't want to be a part of what you do, and now she isn't. I've had to accept what *you* guys do, but she isn't doing it too. Your woman in there - or whoever you end up spending your life with - they will have to accept what *you* do, and that's not the same as just running a ranch."

Max cringed at the honesty of Ash. There was no comparison between Charlie's role in the family business, and Max's. He knew that. He'd just hoped … what had he hoped? Even he didn't know the answer to that question.

"Is it serious with her?" Ash asked, curious. "I've always gotten the impression from Charlie that you like *lots* of women."

"Christy's different," Max said without hesitation.

Ash nodded and smiled.

"Well, that's great then," he said. "I appreciate you thinking that I might be a good person to talk to about this, but really I'm not. I mean, any of your brothers, or maybe your dad ... wouldn't they be better qualified for that question?"

"Yeah, I guess so," said Max. "Okay, well, thanks for that," he continued as he began to walk away.

"Hey! What about the help you offered?" Ash called out and saw Max turn, laughing.

"Yep, you were a great help, Ash!" Max said.

Ash grinned before turning to walk towards the paddock where Tom was waiting. He still didn't like being around the Stonewarden men too much, but had to admit that Max was alright - despite what he and his brothers did.

CHAPTER 14

When he walked back into the house, Max was kind of hopeful that he'd catch Christy saying something about their relationship. His hopes were dashed when he moved close to the door and heard them simply talking about motherhood.

"Wow, that was quick," Charlie said when Max walked into the room. "Just how much help did you provide with the donkeys?" she asked, laughing.

"Didn't need me after all," Max replied before poking his tongue out at his sister.

"Your sister was just telling me the good news," Christy said as Max sat down beside her. A moment later, she realized that he hadn't been told the news. "Oh, I'm so…" she started to say before her apology was cut short as Charlie laughed.

"What news?" Max asked.

Charlie was about to speak when she heard another voice booming in the foyer.

"Anyone home?"

"Oh," Max said, grinning at Charlie and then turning to face Christy. "You're about to meet another family member. Be prepared for this one."

Charlie laughed at his cheeky words just as their father, Mitchell, strolled into the room.

"Hi, Dad," the two siblings said in unison.

"Hey, I hope…" he started to say before seeing the young woman sitting beside Max. "Oh, sorry, you have … a guest?"

Charlie giggled before standing up with Caroline in her arms and moving toward her father.

"Dad, this is Christy," she said, nodding towards Christy while passing her daughter to Mitchell and wondering if Max would speak up and provide any explanation. She was glad when he did just that.

"Christy, this is my dad," he said. "Dad, Christy is … my … girlfriend."

Mitchell held back the laugh that wanted to break free. As much as he could tell that Max was being sincere, he could also tell that the word 'girlfriend' was very unfamiliar in Max's vocabulary.

Grinning in an attempt to hide his thoughts, Mitchell stepped forward a step and held out his hand.

"Hi, Christy," he said. "Max has talked about you. It's nice to get to meet you at last."

Max felt his heartbeat increase. It was rare that he was in an unusual situation that affected him in any way. Within seconds, he'd introduced his girlfriend to two members of his family. Within the same few seconds, he'd used the 'girlfriend' label for the first time in his life. He glanced at Christy, hoping it was okay for him to have described her like that. All he'd been sure about was that he had to call her something, and she was far more than a friend.

"It's a pleasure to meet you … Max's dad," Christy said as she shook the hand of Max's father. Inside, she was confused about the terminology that Max had used to describe her. She hoped he'd been sincere in calling her that. She didn't want to read anything into it. It was far more likely that Max had been put on the spot and felt like that word was what would work best for his father.

Mitchell chuckled as he turned and took a seat beside Charlie.

"You can call me Mitchell, Christy," he said quietly before reclining back and beginning his routine of making his granddaughter laugh.

"Anyway, what was the news, Charlie?" Max asked when he remembered the conversation from before their father's entrance. "You were saying…"

"Oh, Ash and I are going to have another baby!" Charlie said, grinning at her brother and father.

Mitchell stopped his cooing and looked at his daughter with surprise.

"I thought you didn't think you were ready for another one yet," he said quietly.

"I know," said Charlie. "But we've been talking about it and both agree that we are ready. And besides, you look like you need more grandkids."

Mitchell smiled at her.

"What makes you say that?" he asked, chuckling as he cuddled Caroline, making her laugh.

"Congrats," Max said to his sister. She'd already beaten him to finding love, getting married, and having one kid. Sometimes he felt like she was the older one of the two of them, not the other way around.

"Thanks," Charlie said, smiling at him. At any other time, she'd use the timing to tease him about getting on and settling down to have some kids himself. She sensed that the woman sitting beside Max was as uncomfortable in some settings as Charlie had once been. She wasn't going to say or do anything to contribute to Christy's discomfort.

"You're gonna have a baby sister or brother," Mitchell said in a sing-song voice to little Caroline as she looked up at him from her place on his lap.

"It'll be nice for her to have one that's close in age, I think," Charlie said.

"Sometimes that works," said Mitchell. "Sometimes it doesn't. You two are closer than either of you are to Fitz. But you're right. It is nice when kids have someone to play with and spend time with." For a long while, he thought over the years of raising his six kids. No matter how much time passed, he could still remember the day that each of them had been born, as well as all their little and big milestones in growing up. "You might not need Granddad anymore," he joked to the infant on his need.

"Gran-ad," Caroline's timid voice said, making Mitchell smile.

"Dad, you're always going to be needed, by her and by all of us," said Charlie. So many times, she'd wished her father would go out and find someone new to love. She would never push the subject, and she assumed he knew what was best for him.

"Thank you, Charlie," Mitchell said, feeling oddly nostalgic. "You kids are the best part of my life, as are you, little Caroline!" he added before lifting her up and down quickly, making her laugh.

As Max watched the scene before him, of his father and niece, and his sister sitting nearby, he forgot about Christy for a moment. Instead, his mind returned to the sadness of his mother dying, and how much it had devastated everyone who knew her. He knew that life could be cut short at any time. His being shot had added to his belief in that.

Suddenly returning to the present moment, he turned to look at Christy. The look on her face was one of support. There was no judgment about anything to do with the family members she'd met. There was no eagerness to leave, or indication of her wanting to pressure him into anything. As always, she was just herself. That felt like the biggest turn-on Max might have ever had in his life.

"Well, we might leave you and head off," he said to his father and sister before glancing at Christy again and seeing her give a slight nod.

"I'll walk you out," Charlie said as she stood.

"It was nice meeting you," Christy said to Max's dad as she passed him.

"And you, too, Christy," Mitchell replied, smiling at her.

When the three young people had left the room, Mitchell continued his playing and cuddling with his granddaughter, but his mind was active. Seeing Max with a woman was as much of a surprise as seeing James with Sasha had been at the start. Mitchell smiled to himself. The two sons he'd most worried about when it came to settling down and having families themselves, both seemed to be changing their womanizing ways. It was good to see. If Mitchell had his way, every one of his kids would get to experience the love that he'd experienced with their mother.

As he thought about the older and now-gone Caroline, he felt tears begin in his eyes yet again. It was always the way when he thought about his wife. She'd given him so much happiness, and six amazing kids, but then she hadn't gotten to see the result of all of that.

Wiping away a tear that escaped, he smiled at little Caroline on his lap as she pointed to the moisture on his face.

"Tears of happiness, little Caroline," he said before kissing her forehead. "Your namesake - your grandmother - was an amazing lady, and she would have loved you as much as I do."

After hugging her one more time, he resolved to not be sad. He had suffered loss, but he also had much to be grateful for.

CHAPTER 15

At the front entrance to her home, Charlie pulled Max close and whispered in his ear while hugging him.

"It's good to see you found a good one," she said, making him chuckle as he pulled away from her. "Thanks for coming out today, and for bringing Christy."

"It's been really nice meeting you, Charlie," Christy said as she felt herself drawn into a hug as well. "Thanks for having me."

Charlie grinned. Christy didn't look like any of the flings Charlie had seen with Max now and then when they'd been younger. What she did look like was a woman who needed someone just like Max - someone confident but kind. In return, Charlie suspected Max was probably learning a lot about himself at the same time, being around someone so much more grounded than the eye candy he'd previously hung out with.

"I'm sure we'll see each other again," she said, making Max laugh softly.

As Charlie watched her brother do all the gentlemanly things like open the door for Christy, she was happy for him. She remained where she was until they'd started their journey down the driveway again.

"She seems nice," she said to her father when she re-entered the living room. "I hope he keeps seeing her."

"I think he's been seeing her for quite a while," Mitchell said, smiling. "I'm pretty sure she's the one who called him to say the Mustang was ready for him to pick up after…" he began to say before finding that he didn't want to think about his son having been shot. There was still too much rawness about that situation - including who had shot Max, and how that family had started to move into the Stonewarden periphery via James.

Charlie heard and saw the abrupt halt in her father's words. As much as any of them had moved on from the time when Max had been hospitalized in a coma after being shot, it was sad that it seemed to continue to hang over them in one way or another.

"Well, they look good together," Charlie said in an attempt to lighten the mood. "Not exactly the type of girl I've seen him with before, but I liked the way he was looking at her. I'm hopeful about my brother!"

Mitchell grinned and nodded.

"I can only hope that all of your brothers find a way to be as happy in love as you are, Charlie," he said to her.

"No more concerns about my wanting to marry so young then?" Charlie dared to ask.

"None at all," Mitchell said without hesitation. "You and Ash are fine, aren't you?"

"Yeah, of course," Charlie replied.

"Well, all I see when I look at you is something strong, and you already have this bubbly little one, plus another on the way," Mitchell said. "You might be young, Charlie, but you're doing great. I'm proud of you."

"Thank you," Charlie said, smiling sadly at him.

As always, she wanted to tell him to get on and be happy in love again too. As always, she didn't say that out loud to him.

CHAPTER 16

As the Mustang quietly purred down the long driveway from the ranch house, Christy felt contemplative. She'd never had a boyfriend before. Did she have one now? She found herself worried that she'd read more into Max's use of the word 'girlfriend' than she should. She'd read more into so many situations, only to find nothing had been as it had seemed. She had been working on eliminating negativity from her mind in recent times. Something about hearing that word come from Max's mouth seemed to have pushed back her progress.

"Are you okay?" Max asked, sensing her quietness. "Charlie didn't say anything to upset you when I was out with Ash, did she?"

"Oh, no!" Christy exclaimed, looking at him. "No, your sister was really nice. Your dad, too."

"Cool," Max said. "Is something else on your mind?"

"No," Christy started to say, then changed her mind. "Maybe."

Max chuckled. He'd gotten to know her pretty well. She had moments when she wanted to say something but didn't know if she should. He knew that if he remained silent, she'd process her thoughts further and either say what she wanted to say or keep them to herself. Either option was fine with him. He just enjoyed her thinking things through when she needed to.

After a lengthy period of silence, he looked at her again.

"Do you want to go out and do anything?" he asked, taking a moment to study her face while stopped at the traffic lights.

"Actually, I think I just feel like going home," Christy said. She felt like she was in a weird mood. It made no sense, but it was what it was. She had to be more accepting of herself, no matter what that might mean.

"Okay," Max replied, maneuvering the Mustang forwards again.

When they parked outside of her apartment, he turned to her.

"I'm happy to listen if you want to talk," he said.

"I know," Christy replied, nodding. "I don't think I do feel like talking right now, but thanks," she added as she went to open her door. Sensing his hesitation, she turned to him and smiled. "You coming up?"

"Yeah!" Max said, relieved. Whatever was on her mind, he was happy to sit back and let her guide their time together however she felt wanted to.

Once inside her apartment, Christy began to feel like her usual self again. The way she'd felt at the ranch was still simmering in the background, but she also felt a welcome calm flow over her.

Max watched her and went along with her efforts in being light-hearted. It worried him that something seemed to be affecting her but she wasn't wanting to talk about it. He'd have done anything to help her feel better if he could, if only she'd have opened up to him. She'd never been too much of a talker, but her conviction to remain quiet was curious, to say the least.

He continued to wonder about her mood as they had a light lunch and settled in to watch a movie on her sofa. When it was over with, he saw her sit up, turn to look at him, and then lean in to kiss him. When their lips touched, it felt to Max like they hadn't kissed for a long time. It made no sense, but that was how he felt as her lips and tongue lovingly and curiously entwined with his.

As their kissing grew more passionate, Max switched off his thinking. He had to. He'd been holding back for too long, not indulging in what she'd been asking for, just in case he hurt her in any way. The force with which she was being forward told him she was almost at breaking point as well.

Christy broke away from him and stood up, holding out her hand. She was nervous, but she knew what she wanted. Suggesting it yet again might end up feeling like a rejection, but she didn't care. She was a woman who knew what she wanted. She could, at least, act like one.

"Come with me?" she asked him, gulping in nervousness.

Although she didn't expand on her intention, Max felt like he knew. They'd spent a bit of time in her bedroom, enjoying lots of kissing while fully clothed and not crossing any boundaries. The way she'd just asked that question was different from previous occasions. Without answering in words, he stood up, leaned down, and kissed her.

Christy indulged in the passion she felt in his kisses. When she felt him directing her backward while continuing to kiss her, she put her faith and her trust in him. The younger version of herself wanted to talk to her. It wanted to tell her that she was about to be made a fool of. It wanted to tell her that she was stupid to think that someone like Max Stonewarden - a gorgeous man - would ever truly like her or want to be with her. It wanted to tell her that he was going to use her and then discard her like a piece of garbage.

Inside of her mind, she focused on Max's lips and all the delicious physical feelings that were beginning in her body. Whatever her negative mind wanted to say, she wasn't open to listening to.

When she felt the bed against the back of her legs, she pulled away and looked into Max's eyes. After one last scan of his face and reassurance to herself that he wasn't using her and he wasn't going to intentionally hurt her, Christy found some inner strength. Slowly, she began to undress. It had taken a long time for her to be able to look at herself naked in front of her mirror when she was alone in her apartment each night. Although she couldn't see anything attractive in her shape, she'd reached a point where she could at least concede that it wasn't up to her to make that decision about what Max thought. She was resolved. She would get naked in front of him, and she would be prepared for any rejection he was going to deliver at the sight of her.

Max felt his urgency increase with each item that was removed in front of him. When he'd first met her, he'd always thought about her shape. She wasn't like the other girls he'd been with. She was like a little apple instead - but she'd become *his* little apple, and when she stood in front of him, naked, there was nothing about her body that he didn't want to touch and explore.

Sensing her nervousness, he kissed her to help her relax in her own skin. After a long while, he pulled away and happily discarded his own clothing. When they were both naked, he pulled her close against him and delivered more kisses as he encouraged her up onto the bed.

"Lie back," he said quietly. "Are you alright?" he asked when she looked comfortable.

"Yes," Christy said, feeling her heart beating strong. Watching him looking at her body made her gulp in fear of how he was going to act. When she saw his eyes glance down the full length of her body and then back to her eyes, she did not see disappointment. It produced a weird blend of happiness and surprise. "Kiss me," she muttered, encouraging him to kiss her lips so that she could forget she was fully on display to him.

Max grinned at her.

"Oh, I'm *going* to kiss you," he said cheekily before lightly touching his lips to hers and then pulling away to move his lips to her neck. "I'm going to kiss you everywhere, Christy."

Christy closed her eyes to focus only on the feeling of his lips touching her skin. Feeling him kiss her neck felt good. Feeling his lips and tongue begin to lightly dance across one nipple and then the other was her first moment of intense sexual pleasure. She didn't hold back from moaning at the beauty of it.

Max smiled as he indulged. Reading her body movements and hearing the sounds of pleasure and arousal she was making relieved him. If she asked him to stop, he would, without hesitation. If she continued to sound like she did at that moment, he was going to take his time and make her feel as good as he possibly could.

The feeling of her legs gently being parted wasn't strange to Christy. She'd laid on her bed with Max plenty of times, during which he'd nestled between her legs. Even so, when his head moved downwards, she knew she just had to let it happen and see how she liked it. When his tongue hit its target, she *knew* she liked it.

"Oh," she breathed out as his tongue began a merry dance. She wasn't oblivious to how sex worked and what could be involved. Knowing about it hadn't quite prepared her for just how amazing it did feel to have him caress her like he was. Despite her vulnerability and the newness of it all, it took little time before Christy was overwhelmed with her orgasm.

Max grinned. He'd been turned on by her from the moment he'd met her. Feeling and hearing her climax proved incredible. He was more than ready for whatever came next, but he slowed himself down as he gently pulled away and moved up her body again, kissing each area until he was back at her luscious mouth.

"I…" Christy started to say when she looked into his eyes and saw him smiling so much. "I … I don't know what to say."

Max chuckled as he lay positioned above her but not resting totally on her. If there was a second part to come, he wanted it to be by her choice. If she wanted no more, he was very happy to remain where he was, on his knees and enjoying her kisses.

Christy took some time to indulge in the glorious feelings that came from post-orgasm and Max's kisses. He wasn't pressuring her into anything. He wasn't even suggesting anything. He was being the incredible, kind man that she believed him to truly be. It was with no difficulty in making a decision that she reached into a drawer by the bed and pulled out a box of condoms.

"I've never used…" she started to say, suddenly feeling ridiculous. She hadn't opened the box or figured out how to use them.

Max smiled at her and took things into his own hands. He maintained eye contact with her as he removed the plastic wrapping of the box, pulled a condom out, and then remained still, kissing her more.

"There's no rush, Christy," he said quietly, reassuring her one more time that whatever was to happen, he was okay with.

"I know," Christy said, nodding. "I want this. I want *you*."

Max kissed her again before reaching down and readying himself. Shifting his body so that he was relaxed down onto hers, he continued his kisses, slowly beginning to move forwards. They'd been working towards the moment for a long time. He was in no rush as he inched forwards, a little at a time. When he could feel he was at her entry, he pulled away and looked at her again. He held her gaze as he gently and slowly moved into her.

"Yes," Christy said without thinking as she felt filled up for the first time in her life. "Oh, Max…"

Max monitored her facial expression as he began his slow movements in and out of her. When she pulled his head down and began to kiss him passionately, all desire to go slow dissipated. In a very short period, he felt her moving underneath him as if a natural sexual goddess had taken over.

As much as he didn't want it to be over too soon, the way their bodies were moving together was invigorating to the point where he knew he wouldn't be able to hold back. Max thrust his head into the crook of her neck and felt his orgasm flow over him. He'd had plenty of orgasms. The one he'd just had, he knew would have to be up there as being described as mind-blowing.

After a long while, he lifted his head and looked at her. The smile she sported was glorious, making him chuckle. While kissing her lips over and over, he pulled out, discarded the condom, and then lay beside her, holding out his arm to encourage her to cuddle into him.

Christy smiled, and kept smiling. After relaxing into the crook of his shoulder for a long while in silence, she lifted her head and looked at him.

"I really like you, Max," she said.

"Well, I'm glad about that, considering what we just shared!" he said, half in jest. "What's on your mind, Christy?" he urged her softly as he studied her face.

"When we were at your sister's," she began to say. "You introduced me as your girlfriend."

"I did," Max said, gently caressing her cheek. "Did that make you uncomfortable?"

"No!" Christy said, then reassessed the question. "Well, not uncomfortable, but … maybe uncertain?"

"About what?"

"About … whether you said that and meant it, or you said it just to make your father happy," said Christy, thinking to herself that it was a weird thing to even be talking about. "Sorry, I…"

"Don't say you're sorry," Max said to her before pulling her down for a kiss. "I know that 'girlfriend' is a label, and we haven't had some formal 'label talk', but that *is* how I regard you, Christy."

"Really?" she asked, her negative and disbelieving part of her mind trying so hard to get in and convince her of something different.

Max chuckled but nodded.

"Really," he said. "You - in my opinion, and feel free to argue with this if you see things differently - but you are my girlfriend. You are my *woman*," he emphasized, making her giggle. "You are … you're amazing. There is so much that I like about you. I know you find it hard to accept how great you are, but that is my opinion. I am loving this, Christy - all of this time with you, and doing things with you, and listening to you talk. You are the only woman I want to be doing anything with, so yeah, I'll happily tell the whole world that you're my girlfriend - unless you don't want me to."

"No!" Christy said, unable to stop her smile. "No, I … I like it. I know it's silly…"

Max nudged her onto her back so he could move and lean down to kiss her.

"It's not silly," he said. "Nothing about you is silly, especially your feelings. I always want you to be honest about them."

"Okay," Christy said before feeling his lips on hers again. "I do have one confession to make since we're talking about honesty," she continued, her tone revealing the suggestive cheekiness that she felt inside.

"What?" Max asked, wondering what was going to come out of her mouth.

"Can we do that again?" she asked, making Max giggle. "I liked it."

Max nodded before leaning down and sharing with her all the passion that he felt for the incredible woman underneath him.

A long time later, Christy lay beside him and looked at his face. As far as she could tell, he didn't look grossed out by her naked body. She was pleased.

"Will you stay with me? Tonight?" she asked.

"I'm not going anywhere," Max said happily.

CHAPTER 17

In a family home across the other side of the city, Sasha Leadbetter was lying on her bed, thinking about her ongoing dilemma. For quite some time, she'd been seeing James Stonewarden. It wasn't easy. She was sister to David, who'd been the one who'd shot up the supermarket and, in the process, shot James's brother, Max. Although David had returned to rarely being at home, Sasha felt stressed over the situation every time James picked her up or dropped her off. So far, David's car had never been parked outside at those moments. Sasha didn't believe that luck could continue.

In an effort to reduce the likelihood of James seeing David, Sasha had begun to space out the times when she saw James. As an idea, it had seemed logical. In reality, she missed him when she wasn't hanging out with him. She knew he'd easily accepted that she didn't want to spend as much time with him. That didn't change how much she felt she was doing herself a disservice by acting like she was.

Pushing herself to get off her bed and go seek out food, she saw her mother, Stacey, when she entered the kitchen.

"You're at home a lot right now, Sasha," Stacey said to her daughter. "What's going on with you and James?" she dared to ask. There had been a time when a question could be answered by anything from words to a screaming match with Sasha. Stacey believed those days were gone. Her previously always-angry daughter seemed to have been replaced by a young woman who was mature and infinitely calmer.

"I dunno," Sasha said before seeing her mother approach her at the bench.

"Does this still have something to do with David being back?" Stacey pushed.

"Yeah," replied Sasha as she opened the large pantry and pulled out a loaf of bread. "I think … I don't know. I just don't want those two to come face to face."

"Sasha, if James is in your life, they are going to come face to face eventually," said Stacey.

"I know," Sasha said. "I just … I don't know what to do. David's my brother, but James is…"

"Special?" Stacey offered and saw Sasha nod.

"Yeah," Sasha said. "I do care about him."

"And from what I've seen, I'm pretty sure he cares about you too," said Stacey.

"Hmm," Sasha said, concluding the conversation. She didn't know how to move forward with James while living with the constant paranoia that he'd find out David was back. She'd have to mull it over for longer. "Do you want some toast?"

"No, thank you," Stacey said as she glanced out into the backyard.

"Is Dad home?" asked Sasha.

"No, he's out picking up some things for the camping trip he and I are going on this weekend," said Stacey. "Do you need something?"

"Nah, I just noticed Greg and Rhett sitting out there," Sasha said as she looked out the window also. "Do they *know* that Dad's not here?"

Stacey laughed at her daughter.

"Believe it or not, sometimes people come here to see your old Ma," she teased Sasha, making her at least smile.

When Sasha walked away to take her food back

to her room, Stacey stood where she was for a long time. From where she stood and watched the two men that she'd known since she'd been a teenager, something about their interaction piqued her interest. She knew both of them well, even though she was closer to Greg than Rhett, but there was something different about the way they were sitting, chatting and laughing together.

Hearing the front door open and close, Stacey finally turned her attention around. Seeing her husband, Mark, walk in with a huge bag in his hand made her smile.

"Are we going away for a weekend or a week?" she asked, teasing him.

Mark Leadbetter happily dropped the bag and rapidly moved to take his wife in his arms. After passionately kissing her, he cheekily whispered in her ear.

"I'm horny just thinking about you naked in nature," he said, making Stacey chuckle.

"Well, that horniness will have to wait," she said before pointing out the kitchen window. "Greg and Rhett are here."

Mark kissed her with a silent promise that they'd definitely get to the naked stuff later on. No words were needed for him to express that. Their long marriage had left them well in tune with each other's natures and unsaid meanings.

"Hey, hey," he said as he walked out the back door to where his cousin and close friend sat. "What're you guys doing here? I didn't know you were coming over."

"No worries," Mark's cousin, Greg Leadbetter, said. "We were just doing some tidying up of my place and thought we'd drop in to see how you're going."

"Tidying up your place?" Mark asked. "Thinking of selling?"

"Maybe," said Greg. "Not sure yet, but it doesn't hurt to get the place in order."

"You're not going to take off again and disappear without a word," Mark said in one of his serious tones.

"Nah, I won't do that to you again," Greg replied.

"Good, 'cause I'm taking Stace away camping this weekend," said Mark. "I know the kids are all self-sufficient, but I would feel better knowing they can yell out to you two if they need to."

"Yeah, of course," said Greg.

"You're going *camping?*" Rhett asked, grinning. "You?"

"Shut up," said Mark, not minding the teasing at all. "I want to take Stacey away for a break from this place."

"Is everything okay?" asked Greg.

"Oh, yeah, don't get me wrong. She's happy - well, as far as I know, she is. I just … I just want to do something nice for her, and before the kids came along, she loved camping," said Mark. "She deserves some good to happen to her."

As Rhett heard Mark's words, he glanced briefly at Greg. The two of them had altered their friendship in recent times, but they'd mutually decided that was their business and nobody else's - not even Mark's. For a moment, Rhett was once again envious of Mark and Stacey's marriage. He loved what was happening with Greg, and he had no desire to make that news public, but there was something sad about having made the decision to not share the news with others as well.

"It sounds really good," said Greg. "I've got

camping gear at my place if you need to borrow anything."

"Thanks," Mark said. "I think we're sorted. As long as we have our tent and sleeping bags, we'll be right."

Greg smiled at the thought of his cousin camping. Mark could be as rough as any Leadbetter in the right circumstance, but the thought of him sleeping outdoors amused Greg. He kept his thoughts on that subject to himself.

CHAPTER 18

In the car on the way to Greg's house after they'd left the Leadbetter home, Rhett's mind was active. He liked where the two of them were at, but sometimes he still wanted to fight against it. Occasionally, it put him in a weird mood, and he was very aware of it.

"What's up?" Greg asked, picking up on the silence.

"Do you miss women?" Rhett blurted out without thinking before speaking.

Greg's attention was seized as he turned and looked at Rhett.

"Do *you?*" he asked, curious and mildly amused at the question Rhett had put to him.

"Sometimes," Rhett said, nodding. "I … I do think about normal man and woman sex."

"Yeah, I do too," Greg said in all honesty. "I don't want to not be with you, but there is something about women's bodies…"

"Yeah!" Rhett agreed as they neared Greg's house. "Do … what …"

Greg laughed as he pulled into his driveway.

"Ask the question, Rhett," he said, wondering what his lifelong friend was going to ask.

"Do you want to … pick up a couple of women?" Rhett finally asked. "Like, together?"

Greg turned off the ignition and turned in his seat.

"Hmm," he said, suddenly aroused. "I'm definitely not against that idea, but I do think that before we do anything like that, we need to be brutally honest with each other."

"Okay," said Rhett. "Brutal honesty - I like being with you, I want to keep being with you, I want to be with a woman, and I want to be with a woman *and* you - at the same time."

"You know that if you just wanted to be with a woman, I'm not going to be all weird about it," said Greg. "You don't need to include me…"

"No, Greg," said Rhett. "I have thought about this. I want to be with a woman *and* you."

As Greg watched Rhett express his desires, it felt like someone had turned on an electrical supply in the car.

"A woman each?" he asked.

"Yeah," said Rhett.

"You been thinking about this for a while?"

"I've been *fantasizing* about it," Rhett said, feeling his jeans tighten. "I wanna taste a woman, I wanna sink into a woman, and I wanna watch you do the same."

"Inside," said Greg as images passed through his mind. "Now."

Rhett grinned and climbed out of the car. There wasn't going to be any argument from him about that instruction.

CHAPTER 19

While David Leadbetter sat in the office of the counselor he'd received a recommendation to see, he fought to maintain focus on the conversation at hand. It was his third session with the middle-aged man in front of him. There was nothing bad about the experience of talking about his feelings. He just wasn't sure that any good was going to come out of it.

"How is Kasey's pregnancy coming along?" he heard the counselor ask. David supposed it was a tactic to relax him. In the moments when he felt himself tense up during the sessions, he had to admit that the man he faced did succeed in helping David to relax and start talking again.

"Do you think I'll ever be rid of these thoughts and nightmares?" he asked after he'd indulged in the small talk that seemed required of him.

"Yes," the counselor said without hesitation. "If need be, we can find someone else to help you, but keep working on your exercises, David. I'm sure you will find they help to lessen the frequency of your thoughts until one day you realize you haven't had one in a while."

David nodded. Since the first session he'd had, he'd been following instructions and doing what had been suggested. It had helped a little. What had been on his mind most of the time prior to seeing the counselor had reduced down to only a few times a week. It still worried him that he might have one of his dark thoughts and act on it, but so far, he knew he had to have faith and keep working toward his final goal of being rid of the thoughts once and for all.

"How was it today?" Kasey asked him when he returned to her place.

David welcomed her arms around him and the feeling of her lips on his before he answered.

"It was okay," he said quietly. "I do think it's helping, so I just gotta keep at it, I guess."

Kasey smiled at him as she saw him lower his hand to her belly. She still didn't know the full extent of his family's criminal ways, but she did trust and love David. The way he'd started being gentle with her and paying attention to her growing baby bump added to her faith in him.

"We're due at your parents' place at five, right?" she asked him.

"Yeah," David replied as he looked at his watch. "I'm gonna have a shower before we head over." Concentrating on the bump again, he then grinned. "Join me?"

Kasey chuckled but nodded.

"You betcha!" she said, ensuring she seemed happy on the outside. Inside, she was nervous about the dinner they were going to attend. She had gone to the Leadbetter home once, and David's parents had never even heard of her before. She still felt the sting of that. She'd been with David for so long, but he'd never talked about her - not talked enough for them to know who she was anyway. Kasey hoped things weren't going to be uncomfortable when she met his parents a second time.

CHAPTER 20

Pulling up to his family home, David felt a familiar blend of nervousness and happiness. There was comfort in having grown up there. In most ways, it was still his home. Regardless of the calm he sometimes felt when he was in such familiar surroundings, he also felt apprehension. He knew the deal with the guy that Sasha was seeing. He didn't know when he was going to have to face the guy.

Resolving that it was going to happen sooner or later, he put a smile on his face as he held Kasey's hand tightly in his own and they made their way up the path to the house.

"David," he heard a voice call out from behind them when they'd almost reached the front door. When he turned around, he saw his older brother, Phillip, and his wife, Daisy.

"Hey," David said, kind of relieved that it hadn't been whoever the guy was that Sasha was involved with. "Kasey, this is my brother, Phillip, and his wife, Daisy."

A quick glimpse by Kasey to the two new people told her that they'd almost instantly seen her belly. Neither mentioned it at that moment. That made Kasey nervous. Pushing her slight anxiety aside, she smiled and returned the greeting to both.

Once inside, all were welcomed by Stacey and Mark.

"Sit, sit!" Stacey called out from where she stood at the kitchen counter, serving up the last of the food into large platters.

"Oh, Kasey, these are my sisters, Sasha and Anya," David said in hindsight. "And you've met my mom and dad."

"Hello," Kasey said, glancing around at all the faces. Was she welcome there? She had no idea. Even if she wasn't, she would keep smiling and pretending that she felt at ease, even if she didn't.

"How long till we meet him or her?" Anya asked as she pointed to Kasey's belly, as always being the one person who wasn't shy about coming forward.

"Oh, four months," Kasey replied, subconsciously placing her hand on her bump.

"Do you know what it is yet?" Stacey asked, briefly wondering how it must have felt for Daisy to be sitting so close when she and Phillip had been trying to get pregnant for so long.

"No, it'll be a surprise," Kasey said before feeling David take her hand in his. When she looked at him, she loved the smile he gave her.

"I don't know if this is the right time to tell you this," Phillip said, unsure of protocol. "Umm…"

"You too?" Stacey asked Daisy straight out.

Daisy giggled quietly but nodded.

"Yeah, it took some effort, but it seems the effort might have paid off," she said, grinning.

"Looks like you're going to be grandma to two, Ma!" Anya said as she smiled at her mother.

"And you will be an aunt twice over," Daisy said to the youngest of Phillip's siblings. "As will you, Sasha." She was about to ask Sasha where James was. On remembering the details that Phillip had shared with her about the relationship between the shooting, James, and David, Daisy kept quiet.

"Well, congratulations to the four of you," Mark said, standing up and smiling in pride. "And congratulations to all of us too because we are ready to welcome another generation to the family."

As Stacey smiled, looking up at her husband and then glancing around each of the young faces sitting at the table, she gave thought to Rex. She suspected there would never be a day when she didn't, but the thought of a new lot of little ones beginning to emerge in her life was something to smile about. It was easy for Stacey to remember Rex as a baby, and then as a true rascal of a toddler. While she was happy about all that was happening in the present moment, part of her smile was also due to having had and loved the son that she'd never see again.

"By the way, your mother and I are going camping this weekend," she heard Mark announce, making her chuckle. Even she wasn't sure how that was going to go, but she remained quiet and appreciative of him thinking of it.

"Have you ever *been* camping?" Sasha asked out of curiosity.

"Your father and I used to go camping quite a bit before you lot came along," Stacey said to head off the quips that she could see were about to be aimed at her husband. "If any of you need anything while we're away, you've got each other's numbers, and Greg and Rhett are both in town too, and happy to hear from any of you."

"We'll be fine, Ma," Sasha said before looking at her younger sister. "I'll be here all weekend, so can watch out for Anya."

"I don't need..." Anya started to say in objection. Knowing how much her sister was trying to be cool with her when previously Sasha had only ever seemed annoyed, Anya changed her direction of speech. "Cool, thanks."

Stacey smiled at each of her daughters. How they would get on if left alone in the house together was unknown, but it would be far better than it could have been if Sasha hadn't changed and grown as much as she had in recent times.

"But enough of the speeches," she said, smiling at Mark before glancing around the table. "Everybody dig in and eat!"

CHAPTER 21

"You seem excited," Stacey said to Mark when they were finally on their way out of town for the weekend.

Mark turned in his seat and grinned at her.

"Hell, yes!" he said, unable to contain his enthusiasm. "Just you and me in nature? That's long overdue."

Stacey chuckled and resumed her stare at the world passing outside of the car. It had been a long time since the two of them had been away from their home together, and even longer since they'd camped together. In truth, she didn't mind where they were so long as they were healthy, happy, and together. Still, he'd arranged the weekend mostly to make her happy. How many women could say that about the men they devoted their lives to?

When they reached the forest area where they'd often camped prior to becoming parents, Mark took his time driving around the rugged road till he found a spot that looked good to him.

"Flat, quiet, and secluded," he said, turning to smile at her again. "Just what we need," he added with a suggestive tone in his voice.

Stacey smiled at him, foreseeing what would be just ahead of them as they unpacked and set up the tent and their campsite. She loved Mark, but she was well aware of what tested his patience. Fortunately, over their long marriage, she'd mastered the art of addressing his frustrations with a smile and knowing just how to use her feminine charms to defuse him.

As expected, it wasn't long before the quiet

muttering began under Mark's breath in his effort to erect the tent. Before he got too serious, Stacey walked up to him, removed the tent post from his hand, and stood on her tiptoes to kiss him. That was all it took for her to feel the growth in his jeans as he pulled her close against him. She spoke no more as she happily let him lead her down to the ground.

"We haven't even got the tent up yet," Mark muttered between kisses as he grinned.

"No, but you are, and I fully intend to make full use of that," Stacey said as she lowered her jeans and turned around on all fours, presenting to him a sight that she knew he'd never refuse.

Mark wasted no time. When his wife wanted sex, she wasn't shy about saying or showing him exactly how she wanted it. Without speaking again, he lowered his jeans and nudged into her, making them both moan in the same moment at the feeling of joining.

It took only minutes of hard thrusting before he exploded inside of her. As soon as the feelings of bliss eased off, he pulled out of her, lay down on his back, and instructed her to hover over him. As far as he was concerned, sex was never over until he'd felt and heard his wife climax at least once.

As Stacey felt her orgasm grow, she focused only on the beautiful feeling of his tongue on her. As she'd thought so often during their long marriage, she was once again thankful to have a man who was not only an incredible husband and father but also her perfect match for a lover.

When the rush had flowed over her, she pulled up her jeans, turned around, and then lay down beside Mark.

"I'd forgotten how long it takes for us to put up this bloody tent," Mark said before laughing.

Stacey chuckled and kissed him, feeling like they were the only two people on the planet … and completely oblivious to someone in the bushes watching them with a not-so-happy outlook.

CHAPTER 22

Being looked after by her sister was something that Anya had never experienced before. Granted, she didn't exactly need looking after, but she was mature enough to know that Sasha was putting herself out of her comfort zone in offering to stay at home for the weekend, just in case Anya did need her.

"Where are you going?" she heard Sasha call out when Anya moved to leave the house on Saturday afternoon.

"I'm going over to Yasmin's house to study," Anya said as she walked back towards Sasha's bedroom. "I'll be alright, and if I'm not, I'll text you," she added from the doorway.

"Do I have Yasmin's number?" Sasha asked. She didn't actually want any phone number of any of her sister's friends, but she supposed she should if she wanted to show responsibility.

Anya grinned.

"Sasha, you don't have to do this," she said.

"What?" Sasha asked.

"Act all like parent-y," Anya replied. "Ma and Dad don't even have numbers for my friends."

Sasha smiled but nodded.

"Okay!" she said. "Well, are you intending to be out late? When should I worry if you haven't returned home by?"

"But…"

"Pick a time!" Sasha insisted. She couldn't deny that it felt good to give an order, even though she could see that her younger sister was as amused at her effort as she was.

"Okay! Geez - ten," Anya said. "If I'm not home by ten, do whatever you have to do to find me."

"Done," Sasha said before dismissing the conversation and watching Anya leave her doorway. As an added touch of concern, Sasha moved to her window and watched her youngest sibling walk down the edge of the road until she was out of sight.

Left alone in the house, Sasha lay down on her bed. It was rare for nobody to be in the house with her. Once upon a time, it would have always been Rex who was charging around, definitely not being quiet when Sasha would wish he could be. As she lay still and listened to the peace, she realized it was possibly him that she missed the noise the most of. It had been a long time since he'd left them, but he was still around all the time, she suspected, in everyone's minds and hearts.

The other consideration was that the main reason that Rex lingered in her mind was the connection between Rex having been the suspect in the shooting that had left James's brother in a coma. Everything about the distant connection and the way their two families were linked through it made Sasha think once more that she should just walk away from James. She should walk away and never look back, leaving him and his family in peace without having to think about the Leadbetters ever again.

It was an easier consideration to think about than put into effect. The truth was that James was someone she'd grown to care for - a lot. It didn't seem so long ago that she'd been resolved to never give any attention or anything else to any guy. He'd changed her perspective on so many things.

Just when she was again resolved to give up and walk away from her relationship with him, she threw her arms up in the air.

"Curse you, Pretty Boy James Stonewarden!" she called out while throwing her arms up in the air. She then proceeded to text him to tell him she missed him.

CHAPTER 23

Tent fully set up in their chosen camp spot, Mark and Stacey went to work finding rocks and establishing a fire pit. Once everything was finally in place, they settled in for a quiet night of peace, togetherness, and no distractions.

Feeling Mark's arm around her shoulder as they sat on the ground facing the fire, with a large log behind their backs, Stacey felt secure and calm. Day to day, she thought she was stress-free. The fresh feeling of being completely relaxed out in nature highlighted that she hadn't been stress-free for a long time.

"Happy?" Mark asked, loving how nice it was to be able to switch off to everything and everyone else.

Stacey turned, looked at him, and smiled.

"I am," she said, studying his eyes. "Thank you, my gorgeous, wonderful husband."

Mark leaned over and kissed her softly. No matter how much time they spent together or how many years passed, his heart was always full when he was with her. It didn't matter what they did. They were made for one another. He'd known that from the day he'd met her all those years earlier.

When Stacey felt him pull back from their kiss, she had other plans. There were times when she needed the beautiful sex that they shared together. Other times, however, she liked the act of just kissing. Holding her body back a little, she joined her lips to his again and took her time, tasting and teasing them.

They remained like that, not moving toward anything more, until both heard a crackle in the trees around them.

Stacey pulled back quickly but remained still as she and Mark held each other's gaze. Although no words were spoken, she knew it hadn't been in her imagination. He'd heard it too.

After a few minutes, Mark kissed her lightly again.

"Probably a rabbit or something," he said. "Now, where were we?"

Stacey grinned before resuming her kisses. By the time they stopped, they'd forgotten the noise - until they heard something again. That was when Mark realized that whatever it was, it was bigger than a rabbit.

"Howdy, folks," a man's voice said from behind them, making Mark and Stacey both stand up and turn around. "Sorry to startle you. I've just been wandering the woods, and I saw your fire. Don't mind if I join you, do you?" he continued to ask as he made it clear that he had a rifle with him.

"Actually, we're enjoying some alone time and would like to continue doing so," Mark said, his lifetime of fight-readiness kicking in.

"Oh, yeah, I know," the man said as he continued to look at each of them but began to pay more attention to Stacey. "I've been watching your alone time. Quite the looker you got there," he said, pointing to Stacey. "Mighty fine piece of prime cut of meat."

Mark felt his blood begin to boil in an instant. His instinct was to punch the guy out. The rifle on display made him hold back, at least until the guy outright threatened them.

"I might like a slice of that myself," the guy

said as he took a step closer.

Mark stepped directly in front of Stacey to shield her.

"Step back," he said.

Stacey watched what she could from behind Mark. The stranger was caressing his rifle. There was no doubt it was a movement of threat.

"Step back?" the guy asked, focusing on Mark's face. "I'm the one with the weapon. You look stupid, but I'm sure you're not too stupid to notice that."

Hearing the taunting, Stacey moved against Mark's back and wrapped her arms around his waist. It was her silent signal for him to remain calm rather than lash out in Leadbetter style. It was also her indicator to the stranger that she was with her man, and would only *ever* be with her man.

"It's been a long time since I had some pussy," the guy said, beginning to take steps from side to side. "I bet that beauty back there wouldn't mind a little extra attention, now, would you Darlin?"

"Leave us alone," Mark said, focusing on Stacey's arms and her intention for him to avoid confrontation if possible.

"Hmm, well, see, I could have if I hadn't already seen that lovely pussy," the stranger said. "Now ... well, now I got that image in my head, and yes indeed - I want some of it too."

"You're talking about my wife, and you're not welcome here," Mark continued, finding it increasingly difficult to stand still and do nothing.

"Well, *you* might think that, but does that little lady with the beautiful pussy think that?" the stranger asked, taunting Mark.

"Leave us alone!" Stacey said, already dreading that something horrific was about to happen.

Hearing her voice, Mark instantly regretted his

idea to take her camping. At that moment, he'd have done almost anything for the two of them to be back at their home, warm and safe. While he had confidence in his fighting skills, his fists could never be any match for bullets. The guy was taunting him, trying to make him angry. Mark could hear that in the tone easily enough. For Stacey's sake, Mark did not want to risk doing anything without thinking.

He watched as the guy lifted the rifle and slung it over his shoulder.

"I could leave you alone," he said before smiling at the two of them and then bringing the rifle down enough so that it was pointing at Mark. "Or I could demand what I want. What do you think about that, big guy?" he said as he moved closer to Mark with the rifle continuing to be leveled at Mark's chest.

Mark remained still. It had been a long time since he'd felt like he was in danger. About himself getting hurt, he didn't care so much, but there was no way he was going to let the asshole in front of him touch his wife.

While the guy continued to edge closer, Mark focused. There weren't too many things that he considered himself skilled in, but monitoring a fighting opponent's moves and correctly anticipating the next one was something he'd always excelled in. The tactics might not have been required in recent years, but the knowledge was still in his mind. It was part of being a Leadbetter, and it never went away.

As the guy reached a point where the tip of the gun was almost at Mark's chest, Mark moved swiftly. He'd calculated the best move in his mind. He almost got it right and disabled the guy before a shot could fly.

Almost.

CHAPTER 24

At the home of her friend, Yasmin, Anya happily bounded up the staircase to the bedroom where the two had spent many hours over the two years they'd been at school together. While the friendship didn't have the same length of history behind it as others that Anya shared with a diverse range of kids, there was something about Yasmin that made it easy to be around her.

"So, you get to just hang out with your sister?" Yasmin asked her when they settled onto her bed to chat. "That's so cool."

Anya chuckled.

"Is it?" she asked. "Do *you* like being babysat by your sister?"

"That's different!" Yasmin exclaimed.

"*How?*" asked Anya, almost giggling.

"Because your sister is - wow, she's one cool bitch," said Yasmin, pushing Anya over the edge in giggles.

"One cool bitch?" she asked, teasing her friend. "My sister? You're so weird."

"Well, *I* think she's cool," Yasmin said quietly as their laughter subsided. "I think you're cool too, Anya."

Anya was about to make a teasing comeback when she noticed the difference in the tone of Yasmin's voice. Not sure she'd heard it before, she turned and looked at her friend. When she did, she saw Yasmin lean toward her.

For a first kiss, Anya wasn't sure how to

respond. The one thing she determined straight away was that what was about to happen, she did not mind the thought of at all. As Yasmin's lips touched hers, she felt an overwhelming need inside of her. It was like something had been sitting inside of her, waiting to come out. She had no experience in kissing at all, but her lips quickly found their way. It was only a minute or two before both young women were lying down, kissing passionately.

After a long while, Yasmin pulled back and smiled.

"Wow," she said. "I didn't think … I didn't know you'd be like this."

"Like what?" Anya asked, not at all worried about what had just happened.

"So … hot!" Yasmin said, making Anya laugh.

"I am?" she asked. "I can't say that I've ever felt *hot*."

Yasmin grinned and leaned in to kiss her again. There was no moving forwards toward anything else, but where their lips and tongues were concerned, there was no holding back.

The joy that Anya had been feeling was interrupted as she heard an alert sound from her phone.

"It's probably Sasha, doing the over-protective sister thing and wondering where I am," she said as she leaned over and picked up her phone. After a quick scan of the screen, she sat up quickly. "I … I have to go."

"What's wrong?" Yasmin asked, instantly worried. "Anya!?" she tried to ask, but it was too late. Anya was already running down the staircase and out the front door.

CHAPTER 25

"Where is she?" James asked Sasha as she sat beside him in his car. The two of them had finally caught up with one another after almost a week apart. It had seemed like things were going okay until Sasha had received an urgent text message and, in turn, asked James if they could pick up her sister and get to the hospital.

After a quick back and forth run of messages with Anya, Sasha had the address they needed to pick her up from. As soon as they neared the house, they could see her outside.

"There she is," Sasha said, pointing. She felt hyper and a little in shock after the news she'd received from Phillip. She'd never been good at processing feelings. She wasn't even sure how to feel about what he'd told her.

"Hey," Anya said as she quickly jumped into the car. "I don't understand. What's happened?"

"I don't know the details," Sasha replied. "We're going to the hospital, and we'll know when we get there."

Anya remained quiet for the rest of the drive. Something bad had happened, but she had no idea to what degree.

"Thanks, James," she said when they reached the hospital carpark. She didn't wait for him to reply before jumping out of the car.

James looked at Sasha in the seat next to him. He didn't want to push himself into her family life, but he didn't particularly want to just walk away and leave her feeling abandoned by him.

"Thanks," Sasha said as if that was all the answer he needed.

"I'm here if you want me to come in with you, Sasha," he said, just in case she was withdrawing out of believing he wouldn't be.

Sasha wanted so much for him to walk in with her. She shook her head at the thought of him and David coming face to face. Any time that happened, it was going to be an uncomfortable situation. She wasn't sure she wanted to risk it happening in the hospital.

"I'm fine," she said as she opened the door. "Thanks."

James watched her walk away and catch up with her sister. He knew the importance of her getting to whoever was in the hospital. He could still remember the shock of finding out that Max had been shot, and having to get to the same hospital to see if he'd made it and was alive. The thought of Sasha possibly having something so horrific to deal with was more than James could take. Whether she liked it or not, he wanted to be there for her in whatever way he could be. She could scream at him to leave when he was inside there, beside her. Until she did that - until she told him to get the hell out and keep away from her - he was going to at least try and support her.

After another minute of contemplating driving out of the hospital parking area, he located a park and then started to walk inside instead.

<h1 style="text-align:center">CHAPTER 26</h1>

As Sasha reached the emergency department with Anya, she rushed to the desk. It was only when there that she realized she didn't have any real details. Phillip had told her to bring Anya to the hospital as quickly as possible. He hadn't elaborated on why.

"Sasha," she heard her oldest brother call out to her. When she turned around, she was engulfed in his arms before he pulled away and faced Anya. "Hey Baby Sister," he said with affection. Usually, she laughed that term off. At that moment, she was somber.

"What's happened?" Anya asked, dreading what she might hear.

"Dad..." he started to say before he saw James approaching. He looked at Sasha and directed her attention by the nod of his head.

"I … I didn't ask him in," she said quietly to Phillip.

Phillip couldn't help but roll his eyes at her.

"Sasha, he cares about you," he said. "Of course he's going to want to be here for you."

"But..." she started to say before she caught sight of her other brother, David, entering. As soon as she had both men in view, she looked at Phillip.

"Is this the first time…?" he started to ask her in almost a whisper. When he saw her nod, he closed his eyes and exhaled deeply. "Fuck."

"Hey, I got your text," David said, running towards them and, in the process, right past James, not knowing what he looked like. "What's happened?"

A moment later, Sasha saw James reach her. That both men were in such close vicinity without even knowing it was almost a bad joke. She suspected it would only be a matter of minutes before one or the other realized who the other was. She didn't want that to happen, but she knew she wouldn't be able to stop it. She'd been trying to control that situation for long enough. It had always been going to happen as long as she was involved with James. It seemed that the time had finally arrived.

"We'll go and see how Ma's doing," Phillip said, ushering David and Anya away.

"Why did you come in here?" Sasha asked James. It felt so good but so bad to see him so close to all of her family.

James smiled sadly at her and took her hand in his.

"I get that you have family stuff going on, and we generally avoid all that, but Sasha, if someone's hurt, please let me be here for you to lean on," he said. "Please."

Sasha felt her heart pound. She wanted to wrap her arms around him and let him make her feel safe and secure. She equally wanted him gone from the scene entirely.

"Okay," she finally said, nodding. There were more pressing matters than the horrible connection that David held to James. Given the present circumstance, maybe the two of them might not even notice one another.

As she turned and began walking in the same direction that Phillip, David, and Anya had walked, she felt James slip his hand into hers. It was a simple comfort but a reassuring one. He was there, and he was there for *her* in whatever way she might need him.

Walking into the room they'd been directed to, Sasha finally saw her mother. Stacey was sitting on a chair beside a bed, weeping. Inside the bed lay Sasha's father, deathly still.

"What happened?" she asked her mother as she leaned down and put her arms around her. Her mother had always seemed so strong. At that moment, she looked more like a frail old lady.

"He was shot," Stacey said to all of her children. For a fleeting moment, she registered that James was in the room. Just as quickly, she forgot about him.

"He'll be alright, though, right?" Anya asked as she walked around the other side of the bed and looked down at the peaceful face of her father. "I mean, people survive gunshot wounds…"

"My brother did," James said quietly without thinking. Usually more perceptive and able to control his emotions, something about seeing someone else in a hospital bed, suffering from a gunshot wound, seemed to make all logic leave his mind. "He was in a coma for months, but then he woke up, and he was fine. Your dad will be too."

When he'd finished his unplanned speech, he felt all eyes on him. It was only in that moment that it registered that there was an extra person in the room, who he'd never seen before. Looking at that face, he could tell that whoever that was, they had just reached the same realization about him.

Glancing quickly at Sasha with a silent question in his look, James had to hold back with all his might to say nothing more. Instead of speaking, he turned so he could place all of his focus on her and nobody else. There was no doubt that inside the room with him was the brother who'd shot Max. It was wrong, and there were so many ways that James had dreamed he'd deal with exactly that situation. Instead of reacting outwardly, he looked at the bed. On it was Sasha's father. That was the present. Max having been shot was in the past. James resolved that he had to focus on the present - on supporting Sasha. The other issue did not exist within the walls of the hospital.

While Phillip watched James, ready to intervene if things were about to get uncomfortable, he had to admit that Sasha's boyfriend was more self-controlled than he expected he would have been in the same situation. He saw the moment that James registered who David was. He saw the effort James had to put into remaining still and not saying or doing anything. He also saw the way that James turned away from David so he could focus only on Sasha. In Phillip's mind, James had earned his ultimate respect for keeping his cool.

Having also watched James through the period of discovery, Sasha caught his eye when he faced her. Slowly, she moved closer to him. She was relieved when he opened his arms to her and just held her, saying nothing. He'd said he wanted to provide her with support, and he wanted her to lean on him. She was happy to enable him to do just that. All that she'd been worrying about for weeks was finally out in the open. She had no doubt that they'd be talking about it soon enough. As she leaned on James, she felt relaxed that with the new worry about the health of her father, all concern about James knowing that David was back could be put to rest.

The doctor walking in broke into everyone's thoughts.

"I must speak with Mrs. Leadbetter," he said. "Alone, preferably."

James didn't hesitate to walk towards the door. He wasn't part of their family. He didn't want to know whatever was about to be said. He was relieved, however, when he turned around halfway down the corridor and saw Sasha right behind him. He was even more pleased when she walked into his arms again.

"What if he…?" Sasha started to ask, not trying to hold back her tears. She knew the Leadbetters weren't like a normal family, but her father had always been there for her. She'd known that even when she'd been constantly angry at the world. Not only did she not want to lose her father, but she particularly didn't want her *mother* to lose him. Sasha didn't think there was any love so great as what they had. Her mother … would her mother even survive without him by her side?

"Shh," James said quietly as he pulled her head to his shoulder and kissed the top of her head. "You don't know what the doctor's going to say, and no matter what he does say, anything could happen. They don't always get it right."

Sasha nodded against his shoulder as her tears began to flow. A little way down the hallway, she could see her siblings. She saw each of them glance at her and James, then look away. The one who looked the longest was David. He was also the one who looked the most regretful and like he wished he could crawl away. She was glad he was hanging in there. There was no guarantee that he and James wouldn't come to blows sometime. If they could hold off while where they were, she'd forever be grateful to both of them.

CHAPTER 27

As Stacey prepared herself for whatever the doctor was going to say to her, she knew she was already grieving inside. Mark had lost consciousness straight after his body had taken the bullet. He hadn't woken up since. The time it had taken between Stacey calling for help and the help arriving had seemed like an eternity, but at least they'd shown up while he'd still been breathing.

The moment she had with Mark seemed to last forever as the doctor ushered everyone else out of the room. In reality, it must have only been seconds. In her mind, it seemed plenty long enough for her mind to cast back over the decades they'd spent together. Everyone who'd known her when she'd met Mark had told her that he was a loser and she'd never be happy with him. They'd all been wrong. Sure, she and Mark had their ups and downs, but overall, he'd given her more love than she knew many other wives got from their husbands. His family might not have lived wholesomely, but he had a wholesome heart that Stacey knew had been devoted to her happiness through all of their years together.

"Mrs. Leadbetter," she heard the doctor say, pulling her out of her reverie.

"How bad is it?" Stacey asked, trying to prepare for the worst news possible. "Is he going to…?" she began to ask. She couldn't get the words out. They were too hard to bear.

"You do need to prepare yourself for the worst, Mrs. Leadbetter," the doctor began. "However, the bullet didn't rupture any major organs. I'm confident his body *will* repair itself soon enough."

"Then why…?" Stacey finally asked as her thinking cleared. "Why isn't he awake?"

The doctor held his hands out wide, indicating he didn't have all the answers.

"The body knows what it has to do to heal," he said. "Even though your husband has been lucky in where the bullet entered, the trauma to his body is still great."

"So, you don't think … I know that you obviously don't know for certain and anything can happen, but you don't *think* he's going to die from this?" Stacey dared to ask.

"Correct," the doctor said, nodding. "None of us know how his body is reacting to the trauma or what will happen, but I am hopeful he will wake up."

"Thank you," Stacey pushed out as she felt an overwhelming need to weep flow over her. She held back over the seconds it took for the doctor to lightly pat her shoulder and then quietly leave the room. When he'd gone, she held back no more.

CHAPTER 28

Out in the hallway, Phillip saw the doctor walking right towards him. He confidently prepared himself for whatever he was about to be told.

"Your father isn't out of the woods, but as I've told your mother, I do think his body is going to mend from his wound," the doctor said. "I know you all want to be in there with him, but if you can keep it down to a minimum level of noise and number of people in there at any one time…"

"Of course," Phillip said, nodding. He could feel a level of stress leaving his body. It hadn't been great news, but it certainly hadn't been the worst possible news either. For the moment, at least, it was predicted that his father would live.

"What did he say?" Sasha asked him when she approached.

"He's confident Dad'll be okay," said Phillip. "He did say he doesn't want all of us crowding in there, though."

"I'll…" Sasha started to say. "I'll leave. I can take Anya with me."

"If you want to do that, then go in there now, Sasha," Phillip instructed her. "Go and talk to Ma before you go. We'll wait out here till you've talked to her."

Sasha nodded and began to walk toward the room. She'd taken a few steps before she realized that James wasn't with her. Turning back to him, she held out her hand.

"Come with me?" she asked.

James happily strode forward to meet her and hold her hand, ready to keep providing her with whatever strength she needed.

Inside the hospital room, they were faced by her mother's crying. Although something she'd never have done when she'd been younger, Sasha didn't hesitate to move forward and lean down to place her arms around Stacey.

Feeling her daughter's arms around her, Stacey indulged in the brief feeling of support before she pulled away. It was her job to support her children - not the other way around. When she saw Sasha take a step backward, Stacey noticed James close by.

"I know that your brother was shot," she said to him and saw him nod. "I also believe that it was one of my sons who did that," she continued, holding her head high to face him confidently. Again, she saw him nod. "I can't undo that having happened. None of us can. But I beg you, as a mother, to please not hurt any of my children."

James felt tears threaten as he nodded. One of her sons had shot Max, but she'd also lost a son since then, and now her husband was lying as lifeless as Max had been. For the first time since the shooting, James felt the full weight of forgiveness on him as any determination he'd held onto to get revenge for the shooting dissolved.

"My brother was shot, and I was angry about that for a long time," he said to Stacey. "But he recovered. I don't know why your son did what he did, but I do know that I…" he started to say as he turned and looked at Sasha. "I care about Sasha, and I have no intention of hurting her," he said before returning his attention to her mother. "You have enough to worry about right now in the present. You don't need to worry about anything regarding the past. Neither of you need to worry about anything to do with that. I can't say I'll forget what happened, but I can promise that I won't be acting on the anger I had."

When he finished his speech, he saw Stacey attempt to smile at him. It wasn't a successful effort, but he could see the effort, all the same. She followed it up with standing, walking to him, and placing her arms around him briefly. It wasn't entirely comfortable for James, but he didn't stop her. She was a mother. James knew that if he could have his mother back, he'd do anything for her.

"Thank you," Stacey said as she pulled away and took a step backward, then turned to face Sasha. "Your dad will be okay. I have hope."

Sasha moved forward and hugged her mother again.

"I know," she said. "We're going to leave now so the others can come in."

Stacey nodded and smiled as best she could as she saw her oldest daughter and James leave the room.

Out in the hallway, Phillip approached Sasha.

"Okay?" he asked and saw Sasha nod. "If Anya goes in now, would you be able to wait and take her home with you? If not, she can come back with us…"

"No, that's fine," Sasha said. In truth, she wanted to be alone with James. They needed to talk about the exact subject she'd been working so hard to avoid. It just wasn't the right time for that.

"Thank you," she said to James when they were able to stand alone again.

"For what?" he asked.

"For…" Sasha replied before naturally turning her head and looking in David's direction. "For being here for me and for not making things uncomfortable."

James pulled her into his arms and held her

tightly against his chest.

"Stop worrying about that," he said. "You've got enough to think about right now. Let's just leave that other issue to lie, at least for the moment."

Sasha pulled away, studied his eyes until she'd convinced herself that he was being entirely honest, and then reached up and kissed him.

"Oy! Enough of that!" they both heard Anya call out as she exited her father's room. It was a small thing, but it was enough to make Sasha and James smile, at least a little.

"Ready to go?" Sasha asked her sister.

"Yep," Anya said simply. Inside, she was rattled by the situation with her father. That was a subject that she knew she could openly talk about with Sasha if need be. The other thing that had rattled her that day was her friend kissing her. She wasn't sure she'd be telling anyone about that. She knew she needed time alone to process that before she spoke to anyone about it - even Yasmin herself.

"Thanks for the ride, James," she said when they reached the Leadbetter home. Although she usually liked being around others, she found she was extremely eager to get to her room and be alone.

"You are very welcome," James said as he watched Anya get out of the back seat of his car.

"Do you want to come in?" Sasha asked him. It was a question she'd rarely asked, especially since David had returned. Although she'd worried about the two of them coming face to face, she found relief in knowing that her concern was behind her and she could relax again.

"Yeah!" James exclaimed in surprise. He'd expected to be leaving as soon as she got out of his car. That she seemed comfortable with him going into her family home again said a lot to him.

Once inside, she led him to the kitchen and dining area. She wanted to provide Anya with support if she needed it. Sasha was relieved when she saw that Anya had already taken herself off to her room.

"Do you want something to eat? Drink?" she asked James. As his initial response, she saw him move closer to her and place his arms around her.

"No, I'm fine," James said, enjoying the feeling of her in his hold.

"Okay, I'll just grab a drink, and then we can go hang out in my room if you want," Sasha said, beginning to feel surprisingly light-hearted.

James said nothing but smiled at her. He never quite knew where Sasha's thoughts were going to take her. Finding out always seemed like a bit of an adventure.

When he followed her down the hallway, he saw her open a door and point to indicate for him to go through it.

"I'll just check on Anya," Sasha said, smiling at him.

James nodded and walked into Sasha's room. He'd been in the home before, but never into her personal space. As he walked in, he realized he'd never given any thought to what her bedroom might look like. She'd been angry when he'd first seen and met her. She'd since mellowed greatly. He took his time, walking around and looking at the imagery that lined the walls.

"You okay, Anya?" Sasha asked as she knocked and then opened her sister's bedroom door.

"Yeah, but thanks," Anya said.

"I'm here if you want to talk," Sasha said.

"I know," replied Anya. "I'm cool, but if I do need to, I'll knock on your door."

"Okay," said Sasha before closing the door and

walking to her own bedroom.

"Is she alright?" James asked when he saw Sasha walk in and close her door.

"Yeah, I think so," said Sasha. "Anya's usually the happiest out of all of us. She knows she can knock if she wants to chat."

"No getting carried away for you then," James said, lightening the mood further with his suggestive tone. He was happy to hear Sasha lightly chuckle.

"I'll try to keep my hands off you, but no guarantees," she said before moving up to him, reaching up and kissing him.

As her lips caressed his, James felt far more at ease than he had done earlier. Everything about her body language and tone of voice told him that she was relaxing, at least a little. That was something that made him happy. He grinned as she seemed to change her mind about keeping her hands off him and instead walked him backward to the bed and pushed him down onto it.

"What's going on here then?" James asked, grinning. "You only just said…"

His words were cut short as Sasha smiled and then began to kiss him again as she straddled him. There were so many reasons why she shouldn't have felt happy at that moment, but she *wanted* to feel happy. Whatever she did, she wouldn't contribute to anything changing with her father's situation, or any situation with the rest of her family. What she was in full control of was herself - her actions and her reactions. She'd been worrying about James and David for so long that she'd forgotten how to smile. Before she'd met James, not smiling had been normal for her. Since meeting him and little Nicky, smiling had begun to be a far more normal thing for her to do.

When James felt her pull away, he continued to

grin. He was happy she was on top of him, and glad to have her kiss him, but he could also see a little bit of thought-action going on. She tried to hide it well. With that realization, he took a moment to consider how much he'd gotten to know her over the time they'd been seeing each other.

"Something's on your mind," he said quietly as he watched her sit up. "You don't need to hide it from me, Sasha, if you want to talk."

"I know," Sasha said, smiling sadly down at him before she moved off him and lay down on the bed, facing him. "I've been really worried about you knowing that David was back."

James turned onto his side to face her. When they lay like that, he considered that it sometimes felt infinitely more intimate than if they'd have been having sex.

"Is that why you've kept your distance? You didn't want me to find out?" he asked and saw her nod. "Sasha, he's a part of your family. Don't get me wrong - I've had pretty extreme feelings about finding whoever hurt Max, and this *isn't* an easy situation for me. But I do care about you, and I do feel lucky that my brother not only survived, but has fully recovered. He's fine as, and I know that he has wanted to forget about the shooting pretty much since it happened. Even if I couldn't forgive your family, or at least your brother, I wouldn't go against Max's wishes to let it lie."

"That … that doesn't actually reassure me much," Sasha said.

"I know," said James as he reached up and caressed her cheek. "You can relax, though. If he and I come face to face in any situation, I won't be looking to make things uncomfortable. I wouldn't do that to you."

"But … the cops…" Sasha began to say, wondering how much James could really put up with.

James sighed. He understood her concern there. If he knew that David had been the one to shoot into the supermarket, and he knew that David was back, would he go and tell the cops that in an attempt to have him arrested? In the silence of his mind, he knew it was not only a valid question, but a valid action to take. Even so, he could still only prioritize Max's wishes, and also consider the position that would put Sasha in. He also never forgot that even though Sasha didn't know the extent of his own family's business, he was also a criminal. One thing he would never want was some kind of tit for tat going on with another crime family.

"I'm not going to go to the cops," he said quietly. "Not for that. Don't think, though, that if he went and hurt someone else, I wouldn't."

Sasha processed that statement before she nodded. She knew that James was being more forgiving than most other people would be. James didn't know what David had told her about having dark thoughts in his head. That fact, she would never share. She and James had their boundaries about what they told each other about their families. That was one fact that she'd easily keep to herself. As far as she knew, David was getting whatever help he could with the dark things that had been haunting his head for years. She wouldn't share details about any of that with anyone.

"Fair enough," she finally said. At least she knew where things stood. James had just told her that he would never report David for what he'd already done, but he most definitely would report him if he hurt anyone else. A line had been clearly defined by the statement. Sasha could only respect that. "You can kiss me now," she said to lighten the mood.

James heard the subject change and was more than happy to accept it. Without saying anything more, he moved forward, pulled her hard up against him, and indulged in kissing her, and kissing her … and kissing her.

CHAPTER 29

Day and night for over a week, Stacey Leadbetter stayed in the hospital room of her husband, Mark. Even though she'd always committed to making her children a priority, she knew they were safe enough and mature enough to be alright without her. The thought of being away from the man she'd loved for three decades was something she couldn't bear.

Over the week that had passed since the camping trip that had gone oh so wrong, Mark hadn't woken up. Every time Stacey opened her eyes after napping, she looked at him, hopeful that he would have woken while she'd slept. Every time she checked, nothing had changed.

"Hey, Ma," she heard her youngest, Anya, say as she walked into the room one afternoon after school was done for the day.

"Oh, little one, how are you going?" Stacey asked as Anya threw her arms around her. "How was school today?"

Anya smiled, partially to make her mother feel relaxed and not worried about her, and partially because she knew that if she thought about the moment she'd had with Yasmin, kissing in the girls' toilet block, her mother might sense something about it. That was a conversation she didn't want to have. Even though she knew her mother would be open to talking about romance in general, the time wasn't right. Every day that she saw her mother, Anya knew that her dad's situation was weighing on her mother heavily. She didn't want to add to that stress.

"Boring," she said as an expected reply. "Nothing to report. How's Dad?" she asked as she moved closer to the bed and looked at her father's face. It didn't look any different from the day before, or the day before that.

"He's just the same," Stacey replied, not bothering to hide in her voice the weariness that she felt. She wanted to be positive for her kids. Spending so much time at Mark's bedside left her feeling like even acting positively seemed far too difficult.

"He'll come back to us," Anya said, trying to smile.

"Of course he will," Stacey responded, also trying to feel happier than she felt. "Is everything okay at home? You and Sasha are getting on alright?"

"Oh, yeah," said Anya. "James is there too sometimes. I like him."

On hearing that, Stacey genuinely smiled for the first time in days.

"He's good for your sister," she said. "I think he's a good person. I like him too."

Anya smiled before she pulled a chair up beside her mother and relaxed into it. It was a small routine that had been established that week. She didn't know if it helped her mother at all, but she couldn't see that her being there could do any harm.

After an hour of sitting quietly, something caught Anya's attention. At first, she thought she was seeing things, like something moved only a small amount out of the corner of her eye. When she continued to look in that general direction, she saw what had seemed like movement in her periphery of vision.

"His hand is moving," she said quietly.

"What?" Stacey asked groggily as if she'd been about to fall asleep.

"His hand," Anya said again, pointing. "It's moving!"

Stacey glanced at Mark, assuming Anya was seeing things. After a few minutes, she saw it too. Without thought, she ran out into the corridor and called for someone to come quickly.

Mother and daughter stood back and watched as a doctor did an examination of Mark. When his examination was complete, the doctor turned and delivered a small smile to Stacey.

"It seems Mr. Leadbetter is ready to wake up," he said.

CHAPTER 30

On hearing the news that Sasha's father had finally woken up, James automatically took a step back to allow Sasha and her family to enjoy his return. James was one person who knew exactly how it felt to see someone from their family in a deep slumber, and then also see them wake after a period of uncertainty.

"Hey, Dad," he said as he walked into the Stonewarden family home. Although he didn't live there anymore, sometimes it felt good to surround himself with the familiarity of his earlier years. It was also where he felt close to his mother, even though she'd been gone for so long.

"James," Mitchell said when his son entered the living room. "What's up? Is everything alright?"

"Yeah," James replied as he slumped into the armchair that had been his favorite since he'd been a child. "Sasha's dad just woke up."

On hearing the news, Mitchell was as conflicted as any of the Stonewardens could be.

"Well, that's good news, right?" he asked in an effort to not show what he felt inside about the Leadbetter family.

"Yeah, I know," said James. "It is, yeah. It's … it's messy, isn't it. I don't know…"

Mitchell waited for his son to finish his sentence, or at least give a clue about what he was implying. Instead, he saw James remain still and quiet as if deep in thought.

"Do you mean the issue with her brother is messy?" Mitchell asked. It was a sore subject that always made his blood begin to feel like it was boiling, but the situation was what it was. If his son needed to talk about those people, Mitchell would be the ear that he might need.

"Yeah," James replied simply again. "Ugh, why did I start seeing her? And even more crazily, why did I keep seeing her when I found out that her family was involved in the shooting at all?"

"Well, one thing I know you're generally good at, James, is extracting yourself from women," Mitchell said cheekily in an effort to lighten the mood.

"I *know!*" said James as he stood up and began pacing. "That's all I need to do - extract myself from Sasha. Once I do that, I won't need to think about what her brother did anymore. I'll be able to forget it and move on."

"In my experience, that is the unknown of any situation," said Mitchell. "Yes, you could end things with Sasha, and you might indeed forget what happened to Max, and who did it … but you also might not. Then you could end up wondering why you threw away a girl who you obviously have feelings for, when having done so didn't help you achieve anything except miss her."

James stopped his pacing and looked at his father. Although he didn't live at home anymore, he did respect advice when his father gave it.

"You think I should just keep ignoring what they did then?" he asked, knowing it wasn't a fair question.

"I think that you have to decide what's more important…"

"Max getting shot is important!" James said automatically.

Mitchell stood up and faced his son. He understood perfectly what the difficulty was about the situation that James was in. Straight after the shooting, he'd felt like finding out who'd done it and making them pay as well. It had taken great effort for him to calm down and not focus on those feelings and intentions.

"Of course it is, but you know as well as I do that Max wants to forget about it, and he wants all of us to forget it too," said Mitchell. "There's nothing we can do to change what happened, and whether or not you're seeing this girl, you'll still probably think about the shooting from time to time. What you need to ask yourself is: is she worth it? Is she worth dedicating your time to?"

"I … I like being with her," James said, nodding. "It's hard for me to think about *not* being with her."

"Then I think you have your answer," said Mitchell. "She is a Leadbetter, but she's also her own person. She isn't the one who hurt Max, and I'm guessing she probably couldn't have stopped whoever did. You've known about this connection for a while now. Why is it bothering you particularly now?"

James looked at his father. He hadn't told him that the brother who'd most likely shot the gun that day was back in town. Making a firm decision not to, he diverted the conversation.

"I think Sasha's father waking up after this time in hospital has made me think about when Max was in the coma," he said. It wasn't entirely a lie. It just wasn't the whole truth.

"That's to be expected, I suppose," said Mitchell. "But if you're going to offer or commit to standing by her, then stand by her in whatever happens."

"Yeah, I guess," James said, nodding. "I think I'll head over to the hospital and see how she's doing, but thanks, Dad."

Mitchell smiled and watched his son walk out. When the house was silent again, he lay down along the length of the sofa. It was just one of many pieces of furniture that had been in the house for as long as he could remember. He'd grown up in the large Stonewarden home, just as his kids had. It was a part of their heritage. The sofa held so many memories for him, both as a child and as a grown man with a wife and six kids of his own.

Caroline. His mind cast back to her yet again. The void created from her not still being around had partially been filled by the new little Caroline of their family. It sounded like another new little member of their family would also be arriving in the not too distant future. It made Mitchell feel needed in many ways, but he knew he was beginning to feel lonely. A decade has passed since Caroline had left them. Over that time, Mitchell hadn't had any desire to meet another woman, let alone get involved with one. As he lay on the sofa and thought about his long life so far, he acknowledged to himself that maybe it was time he let someone new into his life after all.

CHAPTER 31

Vic Stonewarden lay on the bed that he shared with Hayley, his partner of over a decade. He was alone in their home and mindful about many things. His father had been introducing him to various aspects of the Stonewarden business. He knew he still had a lot to learn but so far, he was enjoying all the challenges that he'd been presented with.

As far as the business went, his progress was moving along nicely. He believed that his father was fine with the pace of his learning. There wasn't anything about it that made Vic nervous.

Other aspects of his life, however, always seemed to play on his mind. He'd always been a private person, keeping almost everything from his father and brothers. There was no real reason for it. It was just how he'd always been. Hayley was the most important person that he shared almost everything with. She'd accepted his lifestyle. She'd accepted the things that he did for family honor. She'd accepted who he really was because, with her, he could open up and talk honestly about anything and everything.

As much as she was easygoing and accepting of everything about him, the one aspect that Vic always felt bad about was that she was pretty much a secret. Because he'd always wanted to keep his personal life private and not cross family with non-family commitments, he'd initially not wanted to involve Hayley in anything to do with the family. When he'd told her about what they did, she'd accepted that, but when Vic had thought about introducing her to his siblings and father, he'd always felt panicked. He'd grown to love her so much that he had no desire to make her a part of his family. Instead, they'd built their own life together, with some interaction with her family. The result was that Hayley was fully aware of the Stonewardens, but the Stonewardens had no knowledge of her.

"Hey, babe!" he heard Hayley call out as she entered through their front door. "I've got some groceries. Do you think you could grab the rest of the bags from the car?"

Vic didn't hesitate to jump up, greet and kiss her, then go and retrieve the rest of their food. With the thoughts that had just been going through his head, he rushed through the process. Through his contemplation, he'd realized yet again just how important she was in his life.

"Thanks," Hayley said when she saw Vic put the bags on the kitchen table and start putting the groceries away. "Good day?"

"Yeah, but…" Vic began to say before finding his heart beginning to pump harder.

Hayley stopped what she was doing and looked at him. Since he'd told her about his family, she'd gone through many instances of preparing herself for anything that could happen. She knew that his lifestyle could lead to him going to prison. She also understood that his lifestyle could lead to even worse than that. He'd never said that his brother having been shot had been directly related to their family ways, but it had always stuck with Hayley as a possibility. That sometimes left her fearful about something happening to Vic too.

"What?" she asked, suddenly nervous. Throughout their years together, she'd grown to recognize his moods. He was a man who was usually fairly quiet but easygoing. When he looked serious, it usually meant there was important news coming, and it probably wasn't going to be good.

"Can you sit down for a minute?" Vic asked and quietly watched as she moved to one of the kitchen chairs and sat down, her face revealing her uneasiness.

As Hayley watched him crouch before her, she felt her anxiety start to show itself. It rarely did, but whatever was about to be said, she wasn't sure she was ready for, especially if it meant something bad had happened or could happen.

"You are … everything to me," Vic said, almost having to hold back a choke, he felt so emotional. "Everything that I've ever shared with you, you've heard and accepted. You really are the most amazing woman I've ever known." He studied her face, wondering if she might guess what he was about to ask her. Judging by the seriousness on her face, he wasn't sure if she didn't have any idea, or she did have an idea and she was dreading what he was about to do. After taking a moment to gulp and assemble the words in his head, Vic finally spoke. "Hayley, will you do me the honor of becoming my wife?"

Although Hayley heard the question, it took some time for her to process it. While her mind calculated the words, she watched Vic continue to crouch in front of her, smile, and then pull a small box out of his pocket. Seeing him open it up and show her, she saw his grin widen.

"It's okay if you don't want…" he started to say, trying to reassure her that she didn't have to say yes.

"Yes!" Hayley finally said.

"Yes, you don't want to?" Vic asked, teasing her.

"No! I mean yes! Oh, Vic!" Hayley said,

giggling. "Stop teasing me. You just asked me to marry you," she said and saw him nod. "And I said yes. Of course I'll marry you. I … I love you."

Vic tentatively pulled the ring from the box and watched her face, checking to make sure she understood what was happening. When he saw her grinning at him and holding out her hand, he slid the ring on.

As much as Hayley considered she should probably focus on the beauty on her finger, all she wanted to do then was wrap her arms around her man and kiss him with all the love that she felt. So she did.

CHAPTER 32

Mitchell was about to leave the Stonewarden family home when he saw Vic walk in. Although all of Mitchell's kids were welcome at any time, Vic walking in wasn't a usual thing to happen when they didn't have any job to plan for.

"Vic," Mitchell said when they faced one another in the foyer. "What's happened? Are you alright?"

"Yeah," Vic replied. "Um, do you have a minute?"

"Yeah, of course," said Mitchell, curious. "Come and sit down and tell me what's going on."

When the two men were settled in the living room, Vic embarked on his news.

"So … well, I've been seeing someone for a while now…" he started to say. Before he continued, he once again regretted that he'd kept Hayley away from his family for so long.

Mitchell nodded and remained silent, waiting for his oldest son to continue. He had no idea about what Vic did in his life away from their planning sessions and the business. It was pleasant enough to have just learned that Vic was seeing someone.

"I've … I've asked her - Hayley - to marry me … and she's said yes," Vic blurted out.

Mitchell was so surprised that he almost couldn't speak.

"That's … that's great news!" he finally said. "When … do we get to meet this girl?"

"Yeah, that's … actually, Dad, I've been with

Hayley for ten years," Vic said and watched his father's face. He couldn't guess how strange the news must have seemed.

"Wow," said Mitchell. "Ten years?" he asked and saw Vic nod. "You … that must have been…" he said, beginning to think about the timeframe.

"She came into my life just after Mom died," said Vic, nodding. "She was amazing then, and she's been amazing ever since."

"Vic, I'm really happy for you," said Mitchell, determined to not blurt out the questions that were screaming inside of his head. "Have you set a date?"

"No, not yet," Vic replied. "She has family out of town, so we'll work around whenever they can get here."

Mitchell nodded. He knew he shouldn't have been surprised by his oldest son being ready to marry, but it certainly wasn't expected when there hadn't been any sharing about the relationship at all.

"She does know about us - about our family and what we do," Vic said.

"And she obviously can look past that…" Mitchell said, partly as a question.

"Yeah," said Vic, nodding and smiling. "It took me five years to tell her. When I did, she took a bit of time to think about the news, but since then, she's always accepted what I do - what *we* do."

As happy as Mitchell felt at the news, he couldn't prevent tears from beginning in his eyes. It had been emotional enough when his youngest child had married a couple of years earlier. Now his oldest child was getting married too. All of that combined would have added to the incredible pride and happiness he knew Caroline would have loved to have been a part of.

"I'm really happy for you, Vic," Mitchell said.

"Whenever and however you need my support, you know I'm here and happy to help out."

"I know," said Vic, grinning before standing, suddenly eager to get home to his bride to be again. When he saw his father stand, he felt drawn to hug him. "Thank you for being such a great dad."

Mitchell further held back the tears. Silently he wondered if Vic might be thinking about becoming a dad himself. It was a question Mitchell would never ask. If it had taken his oldest son a decade to share that he was in a relationship, the topic of children would no doubt be brought up in time if it was going to.

"Do you want me to organize a family dinner or something so that everyone can meet this mystery woman?" he asked as Vic pulled away.

"Umm, no, not yet anyway," Vic said, still surprisingly wary of introducing his partner to his brothers. "I'll … I think Hayley and I have a lot to talk about first. There is one more aspect of my relationship with her," he continued, feeling oddly more embarrassed by the second part of his news. "She ... she's a mom. Her three kids live with us too."

"So ... you're also ... a stepdad?" Mitchell asked, further surprised.

"Yeah," Vic replied, feeling surprisingly sheepish. "Well, not officially, I guess, but when Hayley becomes my wife, I want to adopt them as my own, if she's happy with that idea. Anyway, like I said, we still have a lot to talk about and sort out. Maybe once we've organized things and we know what we're doing for the wedding, we could have an introduction to the family thing?"

Mitchell nodded as he tried to hide his amusement. His oldest son had lived away from the family home for so long that Mitchell had never really known what was happening in his personal life. He was as elusive as Fitz and as quiet as Regan. There had never been any of the outright womanizing and projection of confidence that James and Max had always had.

After saying their goodbyes, Mitchell was left alone again. For a long while, he remained where he was, feeling rather perplexed about having missed an entire side of one of his son's lives. When he thought about that a little more, he was forced to face the truth that he was just as unaware of what his youngest son did in his time away from the house as well.

Fitz. He was always the different one. That was something that had always surprised Mitchell. Why was it that Fitz was such a contrast to his brothers?

Chuckling to himself, Mitchell stood and moved to make himself some lunch. He didn't know why Fitz was so different from all of his siblings. He didn't know why Vic had kept a woman secret for so long. He didn't know why he himself couldn't let go of the love of his life, at least enough so that he could welcome someone new into it. What he did know was that after much contemplation about perhaps trying to meet someone new, he knew he really didn't want to. He had an amazing brood of kids, and now there was another generation underway. He was proud of all of them, and he was happy. Why would he go and try and meet someone new?

CHAPTER 33

As Mark Leadbetter lay in his marital bed, the sharp jab-like pain he felt swiftly took his mind back to the moment when he'd been shot. Without thought, his hand naturally moved to the spot of the wound. Although it wasn't entirely healed, his body had done enough work for the doctors to be happy with his progress. He'd been very happy to have been discharged from the hospital so he could finish his recuperation at home. While he appreciated the health care that he'd been able to receive in the sterile room, not sleeping next to Stacey just hadn't been pleasurable. Even with her having stayed most days and nights, sleeping in the oversized armchair the hospital had provided, it hadn't felt close enough.

"Hey, you're awake," he heard her voice say as the bedroom door opened and she walked in. "I've got something sweet here for you," she went on to say as she placed a tray with coffee and his favorite cake on the bedside cabinet.

"I *know* you do," Mark said, grinning and raising his eyebrows in an effort to make her smile.

The effort worked. After placing the tray down, Stacey happily sat on the edge of their bed and leaned down to place her lips on his.

"I meant cake," she said to him, grinning as she pulled back just enough to be able to speak.

"You know the saying - have your cake and eat it too," Mark said.

Stacey laughed.

"I'm pretty sure you've changed that saying

from what it actually goes like!" she said, chuckling as she pretended to scold him.

Leaning down and kissing him again, she felt the familiar stirring in her body. It was a form of torture, wanting to be as close to him as they'd always been, while having to be careful not to put any pressure on his wound.

"I want you," Mark said against her lips.

"And I want you, my gorgeous husband," Stacey said as she pulled back further. "But don't even think about trying to seduce me. I'm happy to wait till you get the absolute all-clear on physical activity."

Mark laughed.

"I can just lie here and not move!" he said cheekily.

"Nice try," said Stacey as she laughed with him. "If you're a good boy, I'll help you with your shower when you're ready to get up."

"I'm already up," Mark continued to suggest in his seductive tone. "Come here so I can show you."

Stacey grinned as she encouraged him to sit up in the bed. When he was comfortable, she carefully placed the tray on his lap.

"Seriously, Stace," Mark said between sips. "I'm dying here from wanting you so much."

"You are?" Stacey asked, enjoying their friendly banter. "*Dying?*"

"Aren't you?" asked Mark, frowning in a way that he knew would make her smile.

"Actually, I'm rather enjoying the anticipation of waiting," she said.

"Waiting for what?" Mark asked, his tone suggestive again.

Stacey chuckled. He was a good man, even if he wasn't as funny as he thought he was.

"Waiting for you to drink your coffee, of

course!"

Mark smiled and gladly indulged in the coffee and cake she'd brought to him. It wasn't easy lying in a bed all day, every day, but he knew he was lucky. The instance at the campsite could have gone so much worse.

As he thought about the possibility of not spending more years with the woman he loved, he felt emotional. He wanted to be happy and light-hearted for Stacey. The bullet that had worked its way into his body was a reminder that sometimes things were going to happen that he couldn't control. He felt blessed that he was alive and she hadn't been hurt at all. When he'd gone down, that creep could have forced Stacey in so many ways. Instead, he'd proven to be a coward who'd run away as soon as the gun had gone off and Mark had fallen to the ground.

"You're gonna be okay," Stacey said as she took his hand in hers and watched his face change. "We're both safe, and don't you worry - I'll be riding you again soon enough."

Mark had been in such a darker place in his mind that he spluttered on hearing her words as he'd taken another sip of his coffee. As usual, she knew when he wasn't thinking happy thoughts, and had successfully defused his mood before it got worse.

"I hope that's a sincere promise!" he said, not able to stop grinning.

"It sure is," said Stacey before she carefully leaned over and kissed him again. "Hmm, cake…"

"Mine!" Mark said, teasing her before he thought about all that he was missing. "How are the kids going? I don't see anyone."

"Neither of the girls have been here much," said Stacey. "They have their own lives. Even Anya is hardly here at the moment."

"She better not have a boy hanging around," Mark said.

"She's gonna have romance in her life, and you know it," said Stacey, grinning at his mock seriousness. "She's far too happy to not have someone want to scoop her up."

"All of our kids grown," said Mark. "It doesn't seem that long ago that they were children," he continued, briefly remembering that he'd had five kids - six including the one that had died as a baby. Now he had only four. As his thoughts flowed over him, he felt his throat tense in a guarded choke of holding back emotion.

Watching his face, Stacey saw the way his eyes began to well up. Carefully, she moved the tray and then maneuvered herself loosely into his hold against his unwounded side. When they were comfortable, they remained like that for a long time, both thinking about their journey as parents.

"I still miss him," Mark admitted after a long moment of silence.

"I know," said Stacey. "So do I. But we got David back, and we've gained Kasey and Daisy, plus soon we'll have two babies in the family. I know it's not the same, but there are happy times ahead."

Mark tightened his hold around her and kissed the top of her head as he agreed with what she'd said. He suspected he'd never fully stop grieving for Rex, but she was right. There was a new generation coming along. That would hopefully mean renewed happiness in the family.

"Have you noticed anything different about Greg and Rhett?" Stacey asked, remembering how her curiosity had been piqued when watching the two of them sitting together more than once in recent times.

"No," said Mark. "But I haven't seen a lot of

them since this happened. What do you mean by different?"

"I dunno," Stacey replied. In the back of her mind, she did have an idea, but she didn't want to speak of it. If something was going on like she had an inkling that there might be, that was between Rhett and Greg. If there was something going on and they wanted Mark to know about it, they'd say something. If they said nothing, it wasn't intended for anyone else to know.

"Should I be worried about them?" Mark asked.

Stacey shook her head.

"No, they both seem fine," she said, wishing she hadn't brought the topic up. "Everyone seems fine," she continued, changing the subject. "Even James is here more often now."

"He better be treating her right," Mark said, again trying to sound serious.

"I think they'll go the distance," said Stacey, feeling happier at the thought.

"What do you think it was about Sasha that caught his attention in the first place?" Mark asked, curious.

"Well, whatever the reason, I think they are good for one another," Stacey replied. "They seem to even each other out in a way. I like him."

"As long as he's treating her right, and he's not causing any grief about David, he can stay," Mark said.

Stacey laughed and pulled away to look at him.

"I don't think it'd be up to you whether he stays in our daughter's life or not, grumpy bum," she said, teasing him until she saw him smile.

"What I care about most of all is that *you're* in *my* life, my beautiful wife," Mark said as he raised a hand and gently pushed some stray hairs off her cheek. "We have a great life, don't we?"

"We do," Stacey said as she felt tears begin from the emotion she suddenly felt. Taking his hand in hers and kissing it, she studied his eyes. "There's not a lot that I'd change about my life with you."

Mark didn't ask what she *would* change if they lived the same life again. That was glaringly obvious. If they'd never taken on the entire Leadbetter way of life, and Mark had never stood down from being leader so that Pete Leadbetter could step up, there was a very good chance that Rex would still be alive. Then again, Rex had always been impulsive and looking for trouble. If he hadn't left them that night, he could have already left them anyway through one mistake or another.

"I love you so much, Stace," he said, gulping down a sob that was threatening.

"And I love you," Stacey said before leaning forward and kissing him gently. "Now, how about a shower?"

"Are the kids home?" Mark asked, wiping his eyes as he sported a cheeky grin.

Stacey laughed with him as she helped him up and out of their bed.

"No," she said. "And no, that doesn't mean you're getting any."

Mark laughed before reaching out and welcoming her to move close enough to provide him with support in walking. In his opinion, it didn't matter how or why she was touching him. He was alive, and so was she. Whatever time they had left together in their lives, he knew they'd be fine.

CHAPTER 34

As Vic and Hayley lay together on an early Sunday morning when neither had to get up to go to work, Vic enjoyed how much at peace he felt from just holding her close. Despite how long they'd been together, there had been few times when they'd had notable or long-lasting arguments. They were alike in so many ways, but especially in temperament.

As he turned over to look towards the bedroom window, he felt her move up behind him and cuddle into his back. It was an innocent move but one that always made him smile. Automatically, he lifted his upper arm in anticipation of hers reaching around him and settling on his chest and then lowered his hand over hers. There were many ways that Hayley had made him feel loved over the years, but when she cuddled him from behind in their bed, Vic felt a particular kind of security.

He lay still in case she was moving in her sleep. When he felt her move and kiss the back of his neck, he grinned with the knowledge that she was awake.

"Good morning, husband-to-be," Hayley said. It had been her new title for him since he'd proposed and she'd said yes.

"Good morning, wife-to-be," Vic replied in turn. It was a strange word - wife. It was also a word that he was looking forward to using to describe how much Hayley meant to him.

"Come here," Hayley muttered as she gently tugged on him.

Vic happily rolled over so that he could face her

and give her the kind of kiss that he knew she loved first thing in the morning.

A long time later, Hayley lay happily in his arms.

"Shall we have the talk with the kids today?" she asked as she lifted her head from his shoulder and studied his face.

"Yeah, if you think this is the best time," Vic replied. "You know I'm happy for all of this to go at whatever pace you want it to, Hayley."

"I know," she replied, nodding. "I think they'll all be happy about the wedding, and I think they'll be cool with you becoming their proper dad too."

"Well, if they're not, that's okay," said Vic. "They're all not far off being independent…"

"Independent?" Hayley asked, chuckling. "Briana's only eleven! She'll be around for a while yet."

"I know," Vic said, grinning. "All we can do is talk to the girls and see how they feel. They don't all have to be adopted if one or more of them don't want to be, right?"

"Yeah, I think that's best," said Hayley. "If they were younger, I'd just make it happen. I think that at the age they are, they should be able to make the decision that they feel is right for them. You're definitely okay with them making their individual choices though? You won't take it personally if any or all of them don't want to be adopted by you?"

"No, not at all," Vic replied. "Nothing much is going to change around here except this finger will have more prettiness on it," he continued, holding up her hand and kissing her ring finger.

"Well, then, we should go and get this done," said Hayley as she felt her heart rate increase at the thought. "We've told them we're all having Sunday brunch together today, so they're all here, probably waiting for food."

"A good time to break the news, you reckon? When they're threatened by hunger?" Vic asked, chuckling. He had no kids of his own, but over the decade that he'd known Hayley, he'd adapted to being a man figure in the lives of her kids.

Hayley laughed softly as she climbed out of their warm bed.

"Are you nervous?" Vic asked her as he got dressed.

"No," Hayley said before truly considering how she felt. "Yeah, a little. I guess … I know that you and I have a good thing. I do believe that my girls all love having you around, but I know that sometimes the thought of it all being legalized and it moving on to marriage does have an effect on kids, even if day-to-day life isn't going to change because of it."

Vic moved to her and pulled her close.

"If they don't like the idea, we'll work through it," he said. "At any time, I can move home for a while if need be…"

"No, I don't want you to do that!" said Hayley.

"I know, but I mean if it means giving the girls some time just with you…" he said. "I just mean, I'm okay with that, just as I've always been."

"I know, and thanks, but let's take it one step at a time," Hayley said as she walked toward the door. "Let's just announce our plans and see what happens."

Vic smiled at her and followed her through to the living areas of their home. Once upon a time, it had been just Hayley's home - a remnant from her previous marriage. Since Vic had moved in, he'd often told her he was happy to contribute to paying off her mortgage. She'd consistently rejected the idea, and he understood why. It was the girls' heritage. It still left him sometimes feeling like he wished they were 50/50 on the home that they shared. Regardless, he respected her feelings and decision, so had stopped mentioning it long ago.

"Good morning!" Hayley called out as they entered the kitchen and dining area. She was pleased to see all three of her girls sitting in the lounge nearby, watching television.

"Hey, Mom," Hayley's fifteen-year-old daughter, Gina, called out as she walked out to meet her mother in the kitchen. "Are we having brunch or lunch?

Hayley grinned at her oldest child's attempt to make a point about how late Hayley and Vic had stayed in bed.

"Haha," Hayley replied as she pulled her daughter close and kissed the top of her head. "Let's get this party started. You wanna make your famous choc chip waffles, and I'll do the rest?"

"Yeah, okay," Gina said in her new teenage mope mode.

As Vic flitted around getting the dining table ready, making coffee, and preparing juice, now and then he caught Hayley's eye. They said nothing with words, but he loved how she looked at that moment. If she was still as nervous as she'd sounded when they'd been alone, she wasn't showing it at all. Vic was impressed and relieved by that.

"Right, everyone, come and sit down!" Hayley called out when the table was set and everything had been prepared.

When her girls had sat down, she gave them time to warm up in conversation. A good half hour passed as they chatted about different things. It wasn't always easy to coordinate everyone being in the same place at the same time. Hayley was glad that they'd found a time when nobody needed to be anywhere other than home.

As the girls continued to chat, she watched Vic. As always, he was just as involved in their conversation, being supportive in anything they were talking seriously about, and teasing them when there was an opening to do so. He'd been incredible to her throughout their decade together. It had been a big thing when they'd met, with her having not only three kids, but one that was only a baby at the time. Hayley never forgot just how incredible he was as a man to have so easily fitted into her family while not having kids of his own.

Watching his face in animation as he chatted away and laughed, she pondered that thought - Vic had no kids of his own. If they married, he possibly never would. Did he want a child of his own blood? It wasn't something they'd ever talked about, and it wasn't a question that Hayley had ever asked. For a moment, she considered the possibility - would she be keen to have another baby? Her youngest was already eleven. Although the thought lodged itself in her mind, she pushed it aside. Maybe that was something they needed to discuss at a later time. It wasn't currently the right time for such a discussion.

"Sooooo, what's this really about?" Gina asked, looking from Hayley to Vic and then back again. "I mean, these waffles are spectacular, if I do say so myself, but … what's going on?"

Hayley grinned.

"You're right, Gina," she said. "Vic and I did want to talk to all of you together."

"Are you having a baby?" Hayley's second daughter, Emma, asked. "Bindy's mom just had a baby. It's all squidgy and looks funny."

Hayley chuckled.

"I'm not having a baby, Emma," she said as she reached out and placed her hand over Vic's on the table. "Vic has … asked me to marry him. I've said yes, but we both want to be sure about how you guys feel about that."

She watched the faces of each of her daughters before she saw Gina shrug.

"Will our lives change?" she asked.

"Will we have to move?" asked Emma.

"Can we get a pony?" asked Briana.

"No," Hayley said as she pointed to Gina. "No," she said again as she pointed to Emma. "And no," she said as she pointed to Briana. "Day to day, everything will be the same. We're staying here, living together just as we are now."

"Okay," said Gina. "That's cool with me then."

"And me," added Emma.

"And me!" added Briana.

"Thank you," Hayley said, glancing around each of their faces again. "There is one other aspect of this that we want to talk to you about. Before I say what it is, I want each of you to, first of all, understand that what we're suggesting, you can each make a decision about. This isn't an all-or-nothing thing. You each, individually, can say yes, or you can say no. It's up to you, and we're just as okay with the yes's as we'll be with the no's."

"What is it?" Emma asked.

"Vic … would like … if *you* like … to legally adopt you so that he'll be your father," Hayley said, taking her time so she could watch each face.

"We already have a father … somewhere," Gina muttered.

"You do," Hayley said quietly. "And if that makes you uncomfortable about Vic claiming that title, that's okay, Gina." She looked around the table, waiting for any other remarks or questions. There were none.

"You guys can take as long as you like to think about this," Vic said, encouraging them all to look up at him. "I would be honored to be able to say I'm your dad, but if you don't think it's right for you, nothing will change or be different."

"Okay," Gina said, nodding. She didn't elaborate on whether she was saying okay to what he'd just said, or okay to the idea.

"So, let's leave that idea just floating for the moment," Hayley said. "What we do need to think about is a wedding."

"Can I be your bridesmaid?" Gina asked, her face instantly brightening.

"Actually, I was hoping you might like to be one step higher than that and be my matron of honor," Hayley said.

"Really?" Gina asked, grinning. "Don't I have to be like old and married for that?"

"My wedding, my rules," Hayley said, enjoying the joy she could see on her oldest daughter's face.

"What about me?" asked Emma.

"And me?" asked Briana.

"You," Hayley said as she pointed to her youngest. "Will be my flower girl. You'll get the important job of throwing rose petals down along the aisle."

"Yay!" Briana said as she jumped up and down in her chair, clapping.

"And you, Emma, will be my bridesmaid," Hayley said to her middle daughter.

She watched all three faces of her daughters grow excited. It was good to see, and a relief.

"Will we have to dance with ... boys?" Gina asked, making Vic and Hayley chuckle.

"It is traditional that the matron of honor dances with the best man, but we can see how that goes," Vic said, smiling at her. "What matters most to me is that your mom has agreed to marry me and that all of you are okay with it. We want our wedding day to just be fun, not seriousness. We want you guys to have as much fun as everyone else."

"Will Grandma be there?" Gina asked.

Hayley nodded smiled sadly at her daughter before responding.

"I hope so," she said. "We wanted to talk to you about all of this first and see how you're each feeling about it before we start actually planning the wedding, but yes, if you're all good, I'll call Grandma and ask her if she'll come."

"Yay!" Emma exclaimed as she threw a punch in the air. "Can we go now?"

Hayley nodded and watched as all three of her daughters grabbed their plates and took them into the kitchen before they disappeared out of sight altogether.

"Well, that went pretty well, I think," she said as she turned to face Vic. "Hopefully, they are all as happy as they looked."

Vic squeezed her hand and leaned forward to kiss her lips softly.

"See how you go with your mom," he said. "It might be a while till we can coordinate her being here anyway. The girls know what we're hoping to do. If they're unsure, hopefully they'll come to you and talk to you about it before the big day."

"The big day," Hayley repeated as she stood, encouraged Vic to move his dining chair back a little, and then straddled him. "Every day feels like a big day with you."

Vic grinned as he pulled her head down and

kissed her.

"Must be your day for dishes duty then," he said cheekily in an effort to make her laugh.

"As if," Hayley said, chuckling as she climbed off him. "They're all yours, Stonewarden."

As Vic happily began his job of cleanup, his thoughts turned to his family and the conversation he'd had with his father.

"Hey," he called out to Hayley as she was about to leave the room. "Sometime soon, will you come with me to meet everyone in my family - before the wedding, I mean. I know my dad wants to organize a dinner or something so everyone can meet you."

Hayley grinned. Something she'd never wanted to do was push herself on Vic's family. In her opinion, if he didn't introduce her to his family members, there must have been a reason behind it. His asking to introduce her, therefore, felt like a huge deal. Happily, she walked back into the kitchen, reached up, and kissed him.

"Yes, please," she said.

No more words were needed.

CHAPTER 35

At the Stonewarden ranch a couple of weeks later, Charlie and Ash were adding the finishing touches to the long table they'd set up in one of the dining rooms.

"Wow, this feels really formal," Ash teased Charlie as he watched her fiddle with glasses and cutlery. It was quite a sight considering how much of a klutz she'd said she was when he'd first met her.

Charlie grinned at him.

"I want everything to be perfect," she said. "I've never met anyone who Vic was involved with."

"Really?" Ash asked. "But he's your brother."

"Yeah, but he's a lot older than me," Charlie said. "He was pretty much out the door before I was old enough to know anything, and he's never been one to talk much. Honestly, I really don't know much about my oldest brother at all."

"Wow," Ash said. Being an only child, learning about the Stonewarden family had provided ongoing insight into so many aspects of family life that Ash had been oblivious to.

"I hope she's nice," Charlie said, her mind casting to the mystery woman her brother was going to wed.

"I can't imagine anyone marrying someone they *don't* think is nice, Charlie," Ash said, teasing her as he moved closer to her.

"Yeah, I know," Charlie said, giggling. "My brothers all surprise me when it comes to women. Max, James, and now Vic."

"And Regan? Fitz?" Ash asked.

"Oh, I've met Regan's girlfriend before," said Charlie. "She's been around for so long that she was at our house all the time at one point. Fitz? You know I have no idea about anything to do with his life. He's … well, I hate to say it since he's my brother, but he's odd."

"Hmm," Ash said without wanting to weigh in on her observations. He didn't know any of the brothers well, although he had gotten to know James and Max a little from their visits to the ranch. Over time, he'd just accepted that sometimes the Stonewarden men would be in his home and in his view, but most of the time, he didn't have to deal with any of them.

"I think I am done," Charlie said, standing back and looking over the table one more time.

"And you have done very well, my gorgeous wife," Ash said as he moved closer and placed his arms around her. "How are you feeling?" he asked as he glanced down at her belly.

"I don't think I'm far enough along to be showing yet, Ash," Charlie said, not even trying to hide the adoration she felt for him. "But so far, everything feels okay."

As Ash studied her face, his mind cast back to before he'd met her. He could never have guessed that he'd be married and a father so young, but he loved every aspect of both.

"I'm so thankful that you're in my life, Charlie," he said and watched her smile in response.

"I feel the same," Charlie replied before looking at her watch. "We have over an hour before anyone gets here, and Caroline is still asleep."

Ash grinned. He knew her subtle words meant something not subtle at all.

"Ahh, you are thinking I should sweep you

away to our bedroom…" he said.

"Well, only if you wa…" Charlie started to say before she felt Ash bend down, pick her up in his arms, and start walking toward the hallway. "Oh, I guess you want!"

"You guessed very right, my beautiful Charlie."

CHAPTER 36

As Mitchell sat at the head of the long table, he looked around with pride. His daughter, son-in-law, and all of his sons were present. Even Fitz had made an appearance even though Mitchell had wondered if he would. It wasn't a formal Stonewarden meeting of any kind. It was a surprise that Mitchell's youngest son was there, but he was glad he was. Day to day, it didn't matter if the siblings didn't interact. That was normal for most families as they grew up and spread out. For the big family things such as weddings, however, he wanted each of his kids to be there for each other.

"So, you are all here to meet someone who will soon be a new member of our family - Hayley," he said as he addressed all the faces looking at him. "Vic and Hayley have decided to get married, so let's toast to them and make Hayley feel welcome."

Hayley felt overwhelmed at being around so many new people, but feeling Vic's hand holding hers under the table helped. Looking around, she found herself analyzing how the siblings all had little bits of similarity in how they looked. In turn, she could see in Mitchell aspects that Vic had inherited from his father. It was surreal to consider that she'd known Vic for so long and never met any of the people she was in the presence of. She knew he must have had his reasons for not making introductions earlier, but there was a hint of sadness in her thinking at that moment.

While the meal was served and eaten, everyone stayed in their seats. When the food was done with, it took little time for the siblings to approach Vic and Hayley and make at least a little conversation.

"It's about time I wasn't the only girl in the family," Charlie said to Hayley, helping to relax her.

"Nor the only mom, Charlie," Vic said quietly.

"Oh, you're a mom too?" Charlie asked, grinning. "How old are your little ones?"

"Not so little," said Hayley, smiling. "Fifteen, twelve, and eleven."

"And…?" Charlie started to ask as she looked at her oldest brother. As forward as she usually was, she couldn't bring herself to ask the question she most wanted to.

"No," Vic said in reply to the unspoken question.

"I was married before, Charlie," Hayley said. "I already had my daughters before I met Vic."

"Ahh," Charlie said, nodding. "A stepdad then!" she continued, smiling at her brother.

"Hopefully," Vic said.

"Oh, he might not be officially my girls' stepdad by law, but he's as much of a dad as they've had for over a decade," Hayley said. "Your brother is wonderful with kids."

"Maybe there will be some little Vics then?" Charlie cheekily asked, quite over her previous shyness about asking what she wanted to know.

"Hmm," Vic said as he glanced at Hayley. They hadn't discussed the subject. In hindsight, he realized they probably should have before he introduced her to his family.

Sensing her father moving towards them, Charlie used the moment to escape. Whatever her brother's 'hmm' had meant, she suspected she possibly shouldn't have asked the question.

"It's so nice to meet you at last, Hayley,"

Mitchell said, not wanting to stress that he'd only heard about her in recent weeks. "Now that you two have set a date, will many of your family be attending?"

"No, just my mother," Hayley said. "My brother can't make it," she added, not adding that her brother hadn't spoken to her since she'd said she was going to divorce the girls' father - her brother's best friend. "But Mom is sure she'll be here, which is most important to me."

Sensing a source of anguish or unhappiness around the subject, Mitchell only smiled and didn't ask any more.

"It'll be nice to meet her," he said. Although it was still so much of a surprise that his oldest son had been involved with someone for so long, but kept her a secret, he couldn't deny that he felt great joy in the knowledge.

CHAPTER 37

Sasha Leadbetter relaxed back on the sofa at James's apartment, not sure how to respond to the question he'd just asked her.

"You want me to come to your brother's *wedding?*" she asked.

James chuckled.

"Yeah," he said. "Why do you sound so surprised? You invited me to *your* brother's wedding."

"Well, yeah, but I don't even know your family," Sasha said, knowing full well that it wasn't a valid reason. When Phillip had married Daisy, James hadn't known Sasha's family either, but he'd still attended.

"Sounds like you're trying to come up with reasons not to go, but, Sasha, it's okay to just say that you don't want to," James reassured her. "I don't mind."

Sasha took some time to think about her options. She wasn't even sure why she was apprehensive about it. She'd met James's father and youngest brother at the Stonewarden house, albeit fleetingly. She'd been introduced to his sister and brother-in-law at the hospital even before that. Could she really say that she didn't know his family?

"Will it be flash?" she asked. "Will I have to dress up?"

On hearing the question, James's mind was cast back to the night of the gala. That night, he'd seen Sasha dressed and presented like she was a model. If only good memories had been associated with that night, he'd have reminded her of how good she looked in a beautiful gown. With that night also being the night that her brother, Rex, had been killed, James didn't mention it.

"It's a wedding - not over the top, but definitely tidy," he said. "You've got a couple of weeks to think about it, so … just think about it," he added before leaning forward and kissing her.

"Okay," Sasha said against his lips. "I'll go with you, but…"

"But?" asked James.

"Will you stay close to me? I won't know anyone," Sasha replied.

"Yeah, of course," James said, grinning. "I won't leave your side. I'll be your knight and protector."

Sasha laughed softly as she relaxed. It was a state she'd been in more often since the news of David being back in town had been made known. Although she and James had spoken about the shooting one more time since them seeing David at the hospital, a solid line had been drawn. They wouldn't discuss it again.

"Do you think I *need* a knight and protector?" she asked, smiling at him.

"I think," James said as he moved even closer. "I think that you are an incredibly independent woman, and I admire you for that."

Although he'd made the statement with a smile on his face, Sasha allowed herself to feel pride on hearing it. For a long time, she studied his eyes and the way they were glistening with his encouragement that appeared to be wound up with a healthy sliver of cheekiness. Being so close to him and seeing how intensely he was looking at her, the only thing she could do was kiss him.

CHAPTER 38

In an apartment not too far away, a similar conversation was taking place between Max Stonewarden and his girlfriend, Christy. Since she'd returned home from the hospital, Max had continued to remain close to her, even after she'd recovered.

"Would you like to come?" he asked her again after having explained that the wedding was approaching.

"Do you particularly *want* me to go, Max?" Christy asked, uncertain.

"Yeah, of course!" Max replied without hesitation. "I want you there with me."

"Don't you have to be someone important in the wedding party, though?" Christy asked. "Like a best man or something?"

"Nope," said Max. "I'm just a guest, and I'd like you to be my date."

He watched her face as she weighed up the option. He wasn't always as pushy but had learned that sometimes she needed a little nudge at least to get her out of her comfort zone.

"Does that mean we'll have to dance?" Christy asked, grinning.

"Have to? No," replied Max. "However," he continued as he stood up and held out his hand to her. "I do believe that you and I *can* dance together when we're there."

Christy smiled at him before standing up and placing her hand in his.

"I don't know how," she said but loved the

smile he was giving her.
"Let's get on with practicing then," said Max.

CHAPTER 39

When the big day arrived, Vic Stonewarden stood in front of the mirror in his childhood bedroom and couldn't stop smiling at himself. He was about to marry the woman who'd been his support for an entire decade. There was no doubt in his mind, and no wanting to wait any longer. His mood was still joyous when he heard a knock on his door.

"Yep," he called out and saw his father walk in.

"Are you all set?" Mitchell asked as he appraised how immaculately groomed his oldest son looked.

"Yeah," said Vic, continuing to grin.

"Nervous?" asked Mitchell.

"No way," Vic said. "I'm more than ready to make Hayley my bride."

"And the kids?"

"They have as long as they want to decide if they want me to be their dad," Vic replied. "Today, though, they each have a role to play. They're pretty excited about it."

Mitchell nodded. That his oldest son was pretty much a father already was still a huge surprise. Although it burned in his mind that Vic had kept his relationship a secret for so long, Mitchell didn't want to ask why. There must have been a reason, and Vic had always been a responsible and thoughtful person. If he'd felt it was necessary, Mitchell had to respect that.

"Shall we go?" he asked.

"Yeah, I'm ready," said Vic.

Mitchell grinned. He'd seen his baby girl get married. Now he was going to see his oldest child get married too. If only Caroline had been able to see either…

CHAPTER 40

When the vows had been exchanged and Vic and his bride had taken their place on the dance floor, Mitchell sat back and watched the happiness around him. Seeing two of his sons gingerly make their way toward the dance floor with their partners was an unusual sight but a joyful one. Once upon a time, Mitchell would never have imagined Max or James to be one-woman men. He read it as a sign of their maturing, that they both seemed to have committed to someone they highly regarded.

Sitting nearby were Fitz and Regan. Mitchell was pleased that Fitz had made an appearance. That was something that Mitchell never entirely expected when it came to family gatherings that didn't involve the family business. Of more surprise was that Regan was alone. He'd had a girlfriend for years. He hadn't mentioned them not being together anymore, but Mitchell's curiosity was piqued. He made a silent note to ask his third son about it at a more convenient time.

Glancing back at the dance floor, he saw Ash lead Charlie out to dance. That sight made Mitchell particularly happy. They were young, but they were doing great. There was nothing about their marriage that made him wary at all. They both equally seemed to have not only accepted the seriousness of marriage and parenthood, but they seemed to have continued to be able to focus on each other as well. All Mitchell ever saw between them when they were both in his presence was a love that was pure and good.

"Are they yours too?" he heard a woman's voice

ask. Turning toward it, Mitchell was surprised to see the mature woman he'd been introduced to earlier as Hayley's mother, Bree. He saw her smiling at him while pointing at Ash and Charlie.

"Yes, that's my daughter, Charlie, with her husband," Mitchell said before pointing out all of his kids. "And there are my sons, James, Max, Regan and Fitz, and of course you know Vic."

"So many beautiful children!" Bree said, grinning at him as she clapped her hands together.

"Well, I know that Hayley has made Vic happy for a very long time," Mitchell said. "You must be proud."

"I am *very* proud of my daughter," Bree said, nodding. "But I know that she has chosen a good man. Vic has been wonderful not just to her, but also to my grandbabies. They are a beautiful couple. I think they'll continue to be happy together for a very long time yet, those two."

Mitchell smiled at her while taking time to silently acknowledge to himself that she was an extremely attractive woman. It surprised him. He'd considered whether he was ready to move on with someone new in his life. It had been easy to believe that he wasn't. But when he looked at Bree and absorbed the scent of her perfume, he felt the familiar, although almost forgotten, feeling of attraction. It was a surprise, but it didn't scare him as a glaring thought raced across his mind - perhaps it wouldn't be so bad letting a woman into his heart again after all.

~~~~~

The End
~~~~~

OTHER BOOKS
BY
ANN M PRATLEY

POWER MOORE INVESTIGATION TALES
~~ Crime Solving ~ Action ~ Adventure ~~

A POWER MOORE INVESTIGATION TALE
HOONIGAN
ANN M PRATLEY

HOONIGAN

Tristan Clarkson has woken up, over and over, bound to a chair, and unable to see. He has no idea where he is, or why he is in the situation he's woken to. His memory is vague, protecting him from recent events that will eventually haunt him for the rest of his life. He wants to remember, but at the same time, his mind acts as though he really, really doesn't. Initially, he's confused. With each waking, his memory clears that little bit more, as do his senses. He soon becomes aware that the very person who has abducted him, is in the room with him, determined to make Tristan pay for something he can't even remember.

Meanwhile, in a hospital nearby a patient has been taken. With the help of Special Agents Ashley Power and Tim Moore, an investigation begins into where the man has been taken, and who would have reason to remove him. With the patient having already been weak from time in a coma, time is of the essence in finding him alive.

Hoonigan is a blend of crime and suspense, intermingled with the strength of friendship, and the awakening of one father's realization of just how much his son really means to him.

A POWER MOORE INVESTIGATION TALE

RESOLUTION
of
HAPPINESS
ANN M PRATLEY

RESOLUTION OF HAPPINESS

Fiona Thompson - better known as Flo to everyone who knew her - took a plunge and stepped out of her comfort zone and into the world of online dating. With persistence, she found her prince. He ticked all the boxes. He was handsome. He was financially secure. He loved her. He married her.

She was warned by friends and family that there was something off about him. She didn't listen.

Then she woke up cold, inside the darkness of a wooden box.

Join Special Agents Ashley Power and Tim Moore as they investigate the disappearance of Flo, going on a surprising journey that nobody in Flo's world could possibly anticipate.

A POWER MOORE INVESTIGATION TALE
HOME BY THE SEA
ANN M PRATLEY

HOME BY THE SEA

A decade ago, homeless people began disappearing from four neighboring towns. Day to day, the commuters making their way to and from work never took notice of the less fortunate they passed. They didn't notice as the number of homeless reduced. They didn't even notice when entire groups of homeless people vanished.

A young woman, eager to find out where her grandfather disappeared to, began trying to find him. When four police departments dismissed her, telling her that her grandfather would no doubt turn up when he wanted to, she was too young to realize she should pursue the matter further.

Now, ten years on, she's stepped up and pushed harder for something to be done to find not only her grandfather but also the countless other people who seemed to have disappeared around the same time.

Called in to investigate the disappearances, Special Agents Ashley Power and Tim Moore find themselves searching for - and finding - so much more than they thought they would.

A POWER MOORE INVESTIGATION TALE

TIGER IN OUR HOUSE

ANN M PRATLEY

TIGER IN OUR HOUSE

When Alana Templeton goes to do the simple task of hanging her laundry outdoors, she becomes aware that something is not as it should be in her yard. The sound she hears is one that many people might not recognize at first. For Alana, it is, surprisingly, a
sound she's heard before.

Being in the yard, with her toddler in the doorway of their home, she knows the right thing to do is whatever she can to save him. The previous time, she succeeded, but will she this time?

A woman and her infant being put in danger of being attacked by the large animal that has escaped the local wildlife park, not once but twice, prompts an investigation into whether there might be more than just bad luck behind the two events. It seems unlikely that someone could have used such a beast for an attempt on someone's life. Then again, it seems unlikely that the animal would escape its confine and end up at the same location two times in a row.

Sent to figure out what might be behind the strange occurrences, Special Agents Ashley Power and Tim Moore begin to delve into an elaborate and rather unconventional scheme to hurt someone through
an act of revenge.

CHISHOLM MANOR SERIES
~~ Historical Romance ~~

ANN M PRATLEY
Alessandra
Chisholm Manor
Book 1

ALESSANDRA

After receiving news from her parents of a possible
betrothal, Alessandra, an 18 year old with an ingrained
belief that no-one would ever wish to marry her, finds
herself in a love so great that at times she cannot breathe.
Married to someone as inexperienced as herself, she
finds herself on a sexual journey of learning
and exploration.

The combination of their mutual inexperience
contributes to Alessandra discovering a degree of
emotional and physical love that she has
never before realized could exist.

That love will be tested by someone from her past with
sinister intentions. Jealous of the physical love
Alessandra shares with her husband,
he is set on doing whatever it takes
to have the woman he desires,
no matter the cost.

FREEDOM OF FLIGHT SERIES
~~ Shifter ~ Young Adult ~~

FREEDOM OF FLIGHT
CHRISTIAN
ANN M PRATLEY
1

CHRISTIAN
(FREEDOM OF FLIGHT SERIES - BOOK #1)

Twenty four year old Christian Shaw has a good life. He's had a rocky ride with being charged for a crime he didn't commit, but he's come out on the other side, older and wiser. He has good friends who've stood by him. He has a family who loves him. However, there's something about Christian that he's never understood. There's something about him that sets him apart. It has made him not want to get close to anyone.

Now someone's appeared unexpectedly. To his surprise, she's just like him. Even more importantly, she has the knowledge to help him understand more about the strange existence he lives. But is she as nice as she appears, or could she have a darker reason for seeking him out and devoting time to him?

Providing an insight into one man's strange journey of coming to grips with who he really is, 'Christian' tells a story of courage, friendship, and crime solving intrigue.

FREEDOM OF FLIGHT

BRANDON

ANN M PRATLEY

2

BRANDON
(FREEDOM OF FLIGHT SERIES - BOOK #2)

For fifteen years, Brandon McStevens has held himself away from everyone he knew prior to the day he turned fourteen. That day changed his life forever. Something happened to him that he can't explain to anyone. He feels ashamed and embarrassed. The only way he's ever been able to move past that and live has been to find somewhere else to reside.

Since leaving his family home, he has continued to live in a small cave. Nestled high above a small coastal community, he has come to spend most of his time enjoying the ocean … oh, and up in the sky. He doesn't know how it happened. He doesn't know *why* it happened. All he knows is that despite understanding how much hurt he must have caused when he left home all those years ago, he now lives the only existence he can imagine.

He's never met anyone like him. He's never *seen* anyone like him. Until that day when that woman and her dog saw him change, no-one had ever seen or heard of him doing that. To this day he regrets having shown himself like he did. But time passed and it has all been forgotten … or has it?

Certain he's the only one like himself, he's surprised when two people come looking for him … and have much to tell him. Finally, the time will come when he no longer has to feel like a freak of nature … or so alone.

FREEDOM OF FLIGHT
TRINITY
ANN M PRATLEY
3

TRINITY
(FREEDOM OF FLIGHT SERIES - BOOK #3)

A strange series of events have been happening in cities around the southwest of the country. When one bank is robbed on a small scale, it makes the banking professionals and law enforcement curious. When a second, then a third, then a fourth are also robbed without anyone knowing how it's been done, agencies combine resources to begin the search to find out who has been doing it and how.

Trinity Love is a twenty-five-year-old woman who's been surviving week to week, doing what she can to find money for her next meal and a roof over her head. In a unique way, she needs neither. She has a level of survival instinct built into her that should enable her to live a good life on the straight and narrow. That kind of life is one that she's never wanted or sought.

Seeing the latest news broadcast about the bank thefts, Brandon McStevens notices something about it that catches his attention. Talking to his new friends, Kelly and Christian, they decide it might be worth investigating.

1
THE
Golden
DESIRES
ANN M PRATLEY

THE GOLDEN DESIRES
(THE GOLDEN DESIRES SERIES - BOOK #1)

He wanted to escape. They needed to survive.

When Isabella starts to dream of a stranger, she's
awakened inside with feelings she has never felt before.
She knows he's not someone she's ever seen before,
and he is not of her village. He is a stranger, and she's
desperate to determine if he is real or he is a
part of her imagination.

Far away, a businessman desperate to escape the noise
and stress of the city embarks on a journey to find peace
and the solitude he increasingly needs and desires. But
at his destination, he will find much, much more.

REVIEWERS SAY:
*"I found myself drawn to keep reading ... almost as if
reading a compelling action/adventure because the
pacing was so excellent. And... ahem... the love scenes
are quite well written, too ... I look forward to reading
the sequel..."*

*"The concept behind this story was intriguing and very
sexy ... Fireworks and all out romance, followed by
some interesting obstacles, but they are overcome,
because well...it's love. What I loved about this read was
the fairytale like narration with a sci-fi/fantasy kick; it
made me feel like I was part of the story..."*

*"... magical quality was a nice twist, delving into the
realm of fantasy romance ... the author's style was well
suited to the tone of the world she has created. Did it*
leave me hungry for the next installment? Absolutely!"

THE *Golden* SUPREMACY

2

ANN M PRATLEY

THE GOLDEN SUPREMACY
(THE GOLDEN DESIRES SERIES - BOOK #2)

What is lying in wait, eager to destroy them?

Living in an ancient village after having passed from present time to hundreds of years into the past, Trent Solace has been monitoring the health of Isabella following the battle they fought in 'The Golden Desires'. Both feel the entity they thought they'd eliminated might not be gone at all, but instead just hiding.

The unknown entity has proven it knows how to manipulate people, making them think things that they wouldn't have otherwise. It controls the minds and bodies of whoever it invades, leaving the host unaware of what they've said, thought, or done over weeks, months, or even years.

Over distance and time, Trent and Isabella met and fell in love, choosing to live together in the ancient village of peace and harmony. Now they must prepare for a second strike from the hidden enemy.

What is it? What is its end game?
And who is its puppet now?

3
THE
Golden
UNITY
ANN M PRATLEY

THE GOLDEN UNITY
(THE GOLDEN DESIRES SERIES - BOOK #3)

Cesare is the golden child of the village. With brilliant
yellow hair that's unlike the color of anyone else's,
he's a cheerful child who, in the eyes of
some, can do no wrong.

Esmeralda is the product of two biological parents who
have buried deep within them, something that makes
them easy to manipulate by the being that has not given
up on wanting to destroy the ancient village. The young
lass with the blue-black hair captures attention and
intrigues the villagers. When they look at her, they feel
confused. It's impossible to determine why but there's
just something *different* about Esmeralda.

Despite them being opposites in nature and appearance,
the two have grown up together as best friends, just as
their parents did before them. The goodness of Cesare
showers a level of kindness and friendship on Esmeralda
that she cannot turn away from. Esmeralda's uniqueness
has always held Cesare's attention. Between them, they
have found a balance that keeps them together as friends.

But what will happen as they move into their time as
young adults? They are unknowing that they are meant
to be paired, but at the same time, they are meant
to be adversaries.

What does the puppet master have planned now? And
how will these two gifted youth react to someone trying
to manipulate them against their will?

A third strike from the puppet master. Will it win in its
plan of attack this time?

CONTEMPORARY ROMANCE

ANN M PRATLEY
Finding
Himself
Again
ANN M PRATLEY

FINDING HIMSELF AGAIN

In a small seaside area of Sydney, Australia, 28-year-old Tom Santini has recently returned to the outside world after ten long years in jail following an error of judgment in his youth. Readjustment hasn't been easy but luck has taken a turn for him. The woman that his brother, Graham, has been seeing is a woman with connections. Through her, Tom has finally found an employer who will give an ex-criminal a chance to start over. It hasn't been an easy six months since his release, but Tom is learning to face his situation with reality and step up to take responsibility for his decisions.

Settled in his job at Toby's Stop'n'Dine, Tom's attention is captured by a young woman who enters. She's beautiful and alluring but, seeing and talking to her, he can deeply sense her being on the run from something … or someone.

Cat is smart, sexy and a woman who will make him wonder if he does, in fact, have a chance at being happy in love, despite his past. But why does she spook so easily? What - or who - is she on the run from? Tom knows that whatever happens, he has to think before he acts. He is determined to do things differently when it comes to dealing with difficult situations. He's already missed out on so much. He cannot go back to prison.

What can he do to calm and keep safe the woman who he so recently met but already has made a difference in his life? How can he save the woman with a deep-seated passion that drives him crazy…

The woman who understands just how important and difficult it is to find oneself again …

PAINFUL DELIVERANCE SERIES
~~ Obsession ~ Romance ~ Psychological Trauma ~~

1

PAINFUL
DELIVERANCE
ANN M PRATLEY

PAINFUL DELIVERANCE
(PAINFUL DELIVERANCE SERIES - BOOK #1)

She just wasn't made for inflicting pain.

She knows it's nothing abnormal. She knows others enjoy it. But with every new level of pain he directs her to deliver to him, Alexis feels another piece of her soul die. He has wealth and he has power, and she knows he won't easily let her go.

But she has to leave. Escape. Move on. Forget. She has reached her limit of what she can do. The plans are in place to get away. She just has to hope that wherever she goes - whoever she meets - she won't find herself in exactly the same situation again.

DARKNESS OF HEART

ANN M PRATLEY

DARKNESS OF HEART
(PAINFUL DELIVERANCE SERIES - BOOK #2)

She thought he'd stopped looking. He hadn't.

She got away from him to start a new life. She moved on. But in his mind, he still loves her and needs her. He still believes that she loves him. That she is meant to be his. That he is meant to be hers.

He will not give up searching for her. He will not give up *fighting* for her. He will pursue her and stop at nothing to get her back. But it will come at a cost … a sacrifice much greater than he will see coming. A sacrifice that will finally wake him up and bring him back to stark reality.

REVIEWERS SAY:
"… author did a great job of making brief references from the first book. Lincoln, Lexi and Alexis are back, though perhaps the most complex character is Diana … very easy for me to recommend this book with 5 of 5 stars."

"This story continued the journey of Alexis, Anthony and Lincoln while giving us a new perspective into the repercussions of Lincoln and Alexis's relationship: from the POV of Lincoln's wife Diana! I loved her addition to the story … kept the tension of the story just right, balancing the calm new life Alexis has been building and keeping the reader engaged."

"It is a book of courage, the courage to leave everything you know behind, the courage to change, the courage to face your fears, and the courage to face the unknown."

FRIENDSHIP OF DESIRE

ANN M PRATLEY

FRIENDSHIP OF DESIRE
(PAINFUL DELIVERANCE SERIES - BOOK #3)

Tom and Samantha. Feisty friends from childhood who feel like they know each other inside out until the day comes when one of them suggests they go to a BDSM club together, and become formal play partners. Pushing the limits of what each of them can individually stand in their lifelong friendship, they attract and repel like magnets, until the time comes when they must choose how they will relate to one another - and what kind of relationship they will go on to have in the future.

While on this journey of discovery, the two of them meet and make a new friend - Alexis. A young woman with a hidden and secretive past, and a mystery surrounding the relationship she has - or has had - with a renowned business entrepreneur who begins to integrate himself into Samantha's life, unknown to any of them whether he has done it for him, or for her … or for Alexis, being the mysterious link from his past.

REVIEWERS SAY:
"While this book is billed as the third in a series, I would classify it more as a spin-off ... I enjoyed this book. Samantha and Tom's relationship was sweet. Their exploration and experimentation, and how it stressed the boundaries of their (frustratingly) platonic friendship was fun to read about. Fans of Ms. Pratley's first books in the Painful Deliverance series will surely enjoy this more intimate peek into Samantha and Tom's relationship."

ANN M PRATLEY

Knight of Desire

KNIGHT OF DESIRE

Cecily, Azura and Maynard have grown up together from childhood. In many ways they've always felt equal ... except for Maynard being a prince, that is.

After her two closest friends find each other in love and then marriage, taking on the ruling of a kingdom, Cecily finds herself questioning if love is in her future. Over time, it becomes apparent that she certainly has caught someone's eye. He is a knight and he is known to be a rogue, but can the handsome Sir Henry capture the fair heart of Cecily, and push her fears aside?

Knight of Desire is a simple old-fashioned short-read romance. There is no adult content or violence in this story.

ANN M PRATLEY

Blade
of
Envy

A FOUR SWORDS NOVEL - BOOK 1

BLADE OF ENVY
(FOUR SWORDS SERIES - BOOK #1)

They expected quite a different kind of destruction...

In the realm of the House of Mordasini, the three royal offspring of King Maynard and Queen Azura are beginning their journeys into adulthood. As the eldest, Prince Aldin, starts to obsess about his future role as the next king, so also begins an obsession about his younger brother. Torn between wanting to be the one who rules over everyone else, but also wanting the life that is being set up for his brother, Aldin begins a journey of envy that grows darker as time passes.

Meanwhile, as one brother ruminates about the life of the other, their younger sister, Princess Semera, appears to grow ill. In the quiet of her deep slumber, something surprising begins to happen as, from a distance, she unknowingly becomes someone else's focus.

ANN M PRATLEY

Blade of Love

A FOUR SWORDS NOVEL - BOOK 2

BLADE OF LOVE
(FOUR SWORDS SERIES - BOOK #2)

In the kingdom of the House of Mordasini, a future
king is waiting for the day to come when his father
will die. While there's nothing to suggest that King
Maynard will be leaving this world anytime soon, his
oldest son, Aldin, increasingly desires to be
the one on the throne.

With the darkness that has been residing in his soul
since he was a child, ideas begin to flow inside of
Aldin's mind. All around him, there are things
happening that go against his idea of how the realm
should be run. In particular, the realization that his
father has granted permission to his brother, Prince
Iztal, to wed is something that adds to Aldin's hatred
for his brother - a hatred that has grown into
an intense obsession.

While brothers continue to share their volatile
relationship, their sister continues to experience signs
that a beast will soon arrive in the realm, eager to
cause destruction. Everyone thinks they are ready
for the beast's return, but are they?

THANK YOU!

Thank you so much for reading my book, 'Emerald of Wisdom' (Book #5 in the Forbidden Conflicts Series). I greatly enjoyed writing this story and I appreciate your enthusiasm for reading it.

~~~~~

If you would like to make contact with me, please:
Visit My Website
http://authorannmpratley.wixsite.com/writingisbliss

Visit my Bookbub Author Page
https://www.bookbub.com/authors/ann-m-pratley

Visit my Goodreads Author Page
goodreads.com/author/show/14777236.Ann_M_Pratley

Thank you,
Ann M Pratley
~~~~~

www.ingramcontent.com/pod-product-compliance
Lightning Source LLC
Chambersburg PA
CBHW061305210726
48293CB00003B/1121